THE CASE OF THE
DESPERATE DRUMMER

The Case of the Desperate Drummer

A McGurk Mystery

BY E. W. HILDICK

For Brian.

19 3 95

denisebaumkus'.

Macmillan Publishing Company   New York

Maxwell Macmillan Canada   Toronto

Maxwell Macmillan International
New York   Oxford   Singapore   Sydney

Macmillan Publishing Company is part of the Maxwell Communication
Group of Companies.

Macmillan Publishing Company
866 Third Avenue, New York, NY 10022

Maxwell Macmillan Canada, Inc.
1200 Eglinton Avenue East, Suite 200
Don Mills, Ontario M3C 3N1

First edition
Printed in the United States of America

10 9 8 7 6 5 4 3 2 1
The text of this book is set in 12 point Caledonia.

Library of Congress Cataloging-in-Publication Data
Hildick, E. W. (Edmund Wallace), date.
    The case of the desperate drummer : a McGurk mystery / by E.W.
Hildick.—1st ed.
        p.   cm.
    Summary: While performing a routine exercise on witness concealment,
the McGurk members suddenly find themselves trying
to hide a world-famous drummer from some dangerous men.
    ISBN 0-02-743961-5
    [1. Mystery and detective stories.]   I. Title.
PZ7.H5463Casc   1993   [Fic]—dc20   92-22726

*To the memory of young
"Traps, the drum wonder,"
who grew up to be
the most dazzling,
demanding, and dedicated
drummer of them all.*

Contents

THE CASE OF THE DESPERATE DRUMMER

1 The McGurkosaurus

"Wow!" gasped Willie Sandowsky.

"And that's only one-*fourth* of the actual size!" I said.

We'd been working on it for a week. I guess we'd been too busy concentrating on our own sections of the monster to see just how awesome it might look when completed. All except McGurk. He acted like he'd known all along.

"It's a winner!" he said, his green eyes glowing.

"I still say the head's all wrong," Wanda Grieg murmured. She brushed back the wing of long yellow hair that had fallen across her eyes. "Impressive—but wrong."

"The head?" Brains Bellingham snorted. "The body's wrong, too. *And* the legs. *And* the tail. It—it—" He gave his short, bristly hair an angry scratching. "*It's a total disaster!*"

He's our science expert, and at the start of the project he'd made some very careful plans. Exactly to scale.

But McGurk had had his own ideas.

"It looks very *fierce*, anyway," said Mari Yoshimura.

"Right!" said McGurk. "That's the main thing, men. It's big. It looks fierce. And it's obviously a distinct creature."

As the word expert, I, Joey Rockaway, couldn't let this pass.

"The word is *extinct*, McGurk. The stegosaurus is an *extinct* creature."

Brains snorted again.

"Stegosaurus my foot! That's nothing but a—a—a *McGurk*osaurus!"

Poor Brains!

It hadn't even started as a stegosaurus. What McGurk had insisted on first had been the biggest prehistoric monster of all. Brains had spent hours on the blueprint for *that* and here's a copy:

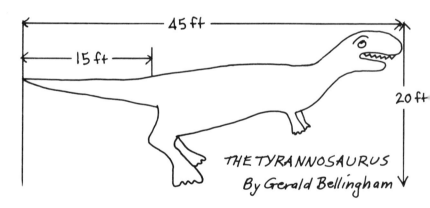

45 ft

15 ft

20 ft

THE TYRANNOSAURUS
By Gerald Bellingham

At first, McGurk had been pleased.

"Terrific!" he'd said. "Even at one-fourth the size it would still be over ten feet long and five feet tall."

"So we'd all be able to fit inside," said Willie.

"Correct," said McGurk. "It'll be—uh-oh!"

"What?" said Brains.

"Are you *sure* its front legs were that small?"

"Positive," said Brains.

"Too bad," said McGurk. "We need one with all four legs on the ground. Four thick legs that'll hide *our* legs when we're walking it in the parade."

So Brains went back to his reference books.

"The saltasaurus," he said finally. "With four thick legs. Okay?"

Once again the drawing was very neat. Very precise.

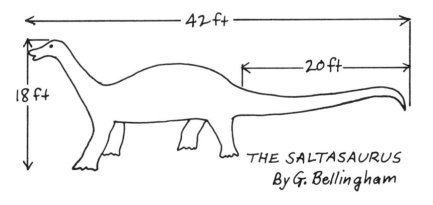

THE SALTASAURUS
By G. Bellingham

But our leader slowly shook his head.

"Nah!" he said.

"But—*why?*" demanded Brains. "What's wrong with it?"

"Too tame!" said McGurk. "Look at that dumb little head. And the tail. Like a pussycat's."

McGurk was leafing through one of the reference books.

"This is more like it," he said. "Something bristly. Spiky. *Fierce.*"

So Brains went to work on the blueprint for the stegosaurus. He didn't take *quite* so many pains over it this time.

STEGOSAURUS
G. B.

"*That's* no pussycat tail," he said, spreading the drawing out. "One flick from that and it would saw a person in half."

"Yeah, but what's with the front legs?" said McGurk. "They don't look so thick to *me.*"

"That's the way they were," said Brains. "The stegosaurus used to reach up and browse off treetops. Nature developed their front legs that way to make it easier."

"It was called natural selection," I said. "Nature developed their limbs for the task over millions of years."

"Oh, really?" said McGurk. "Well *our* task is to win first prize in the Endangered Species Parade. With something really big, spectacular, and fierce. And *we* have only two weeks."

"Yes, but—" Brains began.

"So if *nature* couldn't come up with anything suitable," McGurk said firmly, *"we'll* make the selection *ourselves!"*

And that's just what he did. He selected the body and tail of the stegosaurus, the legs of the ankylosaurus, and the head of something called the dinodontosaurus. Brains flatly refused to make any drawings this time, so here's my own impression of what the creature looked like. After we'd slaved on it for a whole week.

THE McGURKOSAURUS

It didn't look *exactly* like that, of course. When it was at rest, the legs just flopped out limply at its sides. It was only when we got inside and held it up that those thick legs hung down, partly covering ours.

But even in repose the thing looked awesome. And the crazy mixture of old drapes and dresses and our fathers' cast-off suits that we'd covered the thick wire framework with made it look all the more ferocious.

And big—oh, yes!

We'd constructed it in the McGurk garage. Mr. McGurk had gone on a ten-day business trip, vacating his own car space. So when I tell you that the monster completely shut out the sight of Mrs. McGurk's Dodge Aries, right next to it, you can get some idea of its size.

It was some McGurkosaurus, all right!

2 Yoshito

This happened at the beginning of the summer vacation. McGurk would normally have been fretting and fussing because we didn't have a case to work on. But he'd looked upon the coming fancy-dress parade as a challenge.

For one thing, our old enemy Sandra Ennis had told us she was entering the contest as a dodo.

"A what?" asked Wanda.

"A dodo," said Sandra. "An extinct bird. My mom is helping me with the costume, and my dancing teacher is working out a comic dance routine. The Dodo Dodder. It'll knock the judges cold."

When we didn't throw up our hands in awe and admiration, she turned nasty.

"Why don't *you* all go in for it?" she sneered. "As yourselves? The McGurk Organization?"

McGurk looked puzzled.

"How's that?"

"As a bunch of extinct *detectives!*" she jeered. "I hear you haven't been asked to solve a mystery in *months!*"

That was when McGurk decided *we'd* have to do something really outstanding.

Then he heard that another old enemy, Burt Rafferty, was planning to enter the contest with Tommy Camuty as a mammoth.

"Burt's gonna be the front legs and Tommy the back," Willie reported. "And they've got an old hairy rug for the hide and a pair of genuine ox horns for the tusks. Burt says it'll make everything else look like toys!"

That was when McGurk decided we'd have to do something not just outstanding but really *big*.

And besides being stung into action by these challenges, we already had a very special stake in the event.

After all, wasn't the star of the whole thing a cousin of Mari Yoshimura's?

Here's a photocopy of the announcement in the local paper:

DON'T MISS
PERSONAL APPEARANCE
OF

Direct from Tokyo, Japan
with 12-hour nonstop
DRUMMING EXHIBITION

DRUMMER
OF WORLD-FAMOUS
ASAMAYAMA
ROCK BAND

"This Vital Volcanic Virtuoso" —*New Musical Herald*

10:00 A.M.—10:00 P.M. SAT., JUNE 27, at the COMMUNITY HALL
in Support of the
ENDANGERED SPECIES PROTECTION SOCIETY
Admission $3 at the door   Seniors & children $1.50

Anyway, that's how McGurk came to be so full of enthusiasm about the monster.

"It'll be a cinch!" he said, as we gazed at the Mc-Gurkosaurus. "First prize all the way!"

"Hmm!" murmured Wanda. "Not unless we do something about its skin, McGurk."

His freckles bunched up angrily around his eyes. His hair seemed to flare a shade redder.

"What's wrong with the skin?"

Wanda shrugged.

"Well, polka dots and stripes and all those other patterns. It's like a calico cat."

"A *calico*saurus," said Brains.

"We need to paint it green or brown or something," said Wanda. "There's still nearly a week to go."

She turned to the workbench and grabbed a paintbrush from a bunch that was lying there.

"Yeah," said Willie. "A grayish green."

McGurk blinked. It isn't often that Willie is so positive about anything like this. Smells, yes. With *his* long sensitive nose he's a true sniffer expert.

"One moment," said McGurk. "Do you mind telling me *why* green or brown? Or a *grayish green*?"

"Well—that's the color it is in the book," said Willie. His confidence was beginning to fade. "Uh—isn't it?"

"So what?" said McGurk. "How do the book people

know? What evidence is there? The shapes and sizes—
sure. We have the creatures' bones—"

"Fossils," said Brains. "The *impression* of their bones."

"Fossils, then," said McGurk. "What I'm getting at is
this. You can reconstruct their *shapes and sizes* from the
evidence, but there's no evidence about what color their
skins were. And why? Because their skins have crumbled
to dust millions of years ago already."

That silenced us all, for a while.

Then Wanda cleared her throat.

"Well, they wouldn't be like *that*." She waved the
brush at the model. "Whoever heard of animals with—
with polka dots and stripes?"

Sometimes I think McGurk should focus on becoming
a lawyer, not a detective.

"*I* have, then!" he said.

"Huh?"

"Yeah. They call them tigers. And leopards. And gi-
raffes. And zebras. And—you want me to go on?"

"Yes, but—all on *one animal*?" said Wanda.

"They were reptiles anyway," said Brains. "Not animals."

"Reptiles *are* animals," I said. "The word you're—"

"What's *with* you all?" McGurk suddenly roared, looking mad. "Argue, argue, argue! Whose garage *is* this
anyway? Who—?"

He stopped.

Just when this was threatening to become an almighty squabble, the McGurkosaurus had burped.

And I mean *really* burped.

One huge, reverberating hollow burp. Like thunder in the mountains. And from that big weird mouth came the words "Pardon meee. . . ."

They weren't very loud. It was like they'd had to travel a trillion miles.

Then we all turned to Mari, and sure enough, she was grinning.

Mari Yoshimura is our voice expert.

She can imitate dozens of voices. And she can throw them about like the true ventriloquist she is.

She is also one very nice person. She never squabbles herself, and she hates to see us getting mad with one another. I could see straight off that she'd pulled this monster voice on purpose, just to break the tension.

"Aw, cut it out, Officer Yoshimura!" said McGurk, somewhat bashfully.

Then we all stared at *him*. He hadn't addressed any of us as "Officer" for weeks. It's something he only does when we're working on a case or practicing our detective skills. I figured it had to be the mention of detective work in reconstructing prehistoric monsters.

Or was it?

He glanced around at us, looking calmer, more busi-nesslike.

"Forget the monster," he said. "It's fine the way it is. Now, follow me, men. There's something more impor-tant we have to discuss."

Then he led the way across to the side of his house and the basement door at the bottom of the short flight of steps. The door with the notice:

McGURK ORGANIZATION

HQ

KEEP OUT

—followed by the list of cases we had solved.

"Is—is *this* a case, McGurk?" Wanda asked, as he opened the door.

He didn't reply right away. But, judging from the look on his face as he sat in the rocking chair at the battered round table, anyone would have thought that he knew even then that, yes, indeed—we certainly did have a case on our hands.

And not just any old case.

No, sir!

I mean a real live *murder* case!

$\textcircled{3}$ Introducing "Dwight"

"All right, McGurk," said Wanda, when we were all sitting around the table. "Do we have a case or not?"

He widened his eyes, then blinked. He smiled that small, mysterious smile of his.

"Case? What makes you think we have a case, Officer Grieg?"

Wanda glared at him.

"Because it's written all over your face," she said.

McGurk's smile broadened. He was looking very smug.

"Well, yes," he said. "As a matter of fact, we do have a case. Uh—at least a *client*."

"Who?" I said.

"Why—Dwight," he said.

We looked at each other. *I* didn't know any Dwight.

"Dwight *who*?" said Wanda.

"That's confidential," said McGurk. "It isn't even his real name. *That's* got to be kept secret."

Wanda gave a loud, impatient grunt.

24

"*So—what's—the—case?*" she demanded, banging the table with each word.

"Dwight is accused of grand larceny and being a fugitive," said McGurk. "But he swears he's innocent, and *I* believe him." (Here he banged the table himself.) "He escaped from custody, and I promised we'd take his case and prove his innocence. Meanwhile, he's going into hiding."

We gaped.

"Where?" asked Wanda, in what was almost a whisper.

"Here," said McGurk.

He got up from his chair, leaving it rocking. He went across to the wall behind me. He bent over the old, dusty steamer trunk that had been there for years. Normally it acts as a shelf for the Organization's files—the row of cardboard boxes. These had already been moved onto the floor.

"Right here," he said, lifting the lid.

Then he dragged something out.

Something bulky, roughly folded in half.

I thought at first it was a sleeping bag.

Some of the others had sharper eyes.

Wanda gave a little scream.

Willie knocked his chair over in his haste to back away.

Mari made a hissing noise through her teeth.

Brains was grabbing at his glasses, which had slipped off his nose.

And I adjusted *my* glasses and saw—
Well, this:

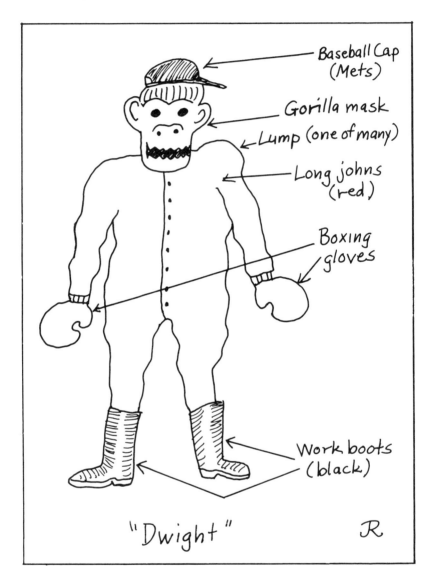

Baseball Cap (Mets)

Gorilla mask

Lump (one of many)

Long johns (red)

Boxing gloves

Work boots (black)

"Dwight"

R

"Meet our new client," said McGurk, sitting him on the trunk, back to the wall.

"It—it's just a dummy!" said Willie, returning to his chair.

"Is this some kind of joke, McGurk?" growled Wanda.

The blood was rushing back to her face, and she looked very, very annoyed.

"Of course it's a dummy, Officer Sandowsky," McGurk said to Willie. "You don't think I'd hide a real person in there, do you? Without air?"

"But what's the *idea*?" said Brains.

"Idea?" McGurk was setting the dummy's hat straight. Then he folded its hands on its lap. "Making the model monster gave me the idea." He had a shot at crossing the dummy's legs, but they wouldn't stay fixed. He let the heavy boots rest flat on the floor.

"But look at that face!" said Wanda. "And *dressed* like that! I mean, boxing gloves! Rubber boots! Thermal underwear! *This* weather! It—it isn't even *realistic*!"

"The gloves," said McGurk, "are so the shredded foam stuffing doesn't spill out of his arms. Same with the boots. The long johns help to give him a human *shape*—something to stuff the cushions and pillows in."

"*Human?*" said Wanda. "With that *face*?"

"Well, I couldn't just leave its head as a bare melon. A melon on a cane."

"Mm! A *canteloupe* melon," said Willie, sniffing. "My favorite."

"Melon-schmelon!" said Wanda. "What does this have to do with a client? An embezzler? A thief who—who's really innocent? Huh? A gorilla in winter underwear!"

"It doesn't have to look life*like*," said McGurk. "Just so long as it's life-*size*. And this is. Five foot two inches tall." He went back to his chair. "Take a good look at it, men. I want each of you to make a life-size dummy of your own. For this very important training exercise."

"Training exercise?" I said. "Training for *what*, McGurk?"

"So we can practice concealing a vital witness," he replied. "Like the FBI does, when there's a big trial and the perpetrator's friends are out to eliminate that witness before he can give evidence."

We were very quiet now. Even Wanda.

"Go on, McGurk," she murmured.

"All good detective organizations ought to have vital witness protection capability," he said.

Well, when he put it like that, we were sold.

Especially when he went on to make a competition of it.

"This is how it works," he said. "We each of us make one and see how long we can conceal it in our homes before anyone discovers it."

"In our *homes*, Chief McGurk?" asked Mari.

"Yes," he said. "Somewhere in the house, or in the yard, but not beyond."

"No problem," said Brains. "At our house we have a big blanket chest and—"

"And that would get you disqualified right away," said McGurk.

Brains's jaw dropped.

"Why?"

"Because although it'll be a dummy, it will have to be treated like a human being," said McGurk. "With air to breathe and enough room to stretch its legs. Also, it will need food. You'll have to take it at least one good meal a day. And"—here McGurk looked very cunning—"you will have to take it to the bathroom at least twice in any twenty-four hours."

"But dummies won't need any food. Or to go to the bathroom," said Willie. "Uh—will they?"

"Of course not," said McGurk. "But they sure would if they were real living vital witnesses."

"A question, McGurk," said Wanda, looking very thoughtful.

"Yes, Officer Grieg?"

"You did say the—uh—vital witness could be concealed on the premises? Not necessarily in the house? Like maybe in the yard?"

"Yes, sure. But—"

"So instead of taking him—or her—to the bathroom

in the house, with more distance to go—wouldn't it be only fair to let him—or her—use a bucket?"

McGurk's eyes narrowed. He thought for a moment. Then he said: "Okay. So long as the bucket is taken to the bathroom *four* times a day. Like you were emptying it and swilling it out."

Wanda sighed.

"Okay," she said. "It's a deal."

"Any more questions?" asked McGurk, glancing around.

"Yes, Chief McGurk," said Mari. "I am sorry, but this week it will be impossible at my house. My mother and the maid will be busy in every room. To get ready for our honored guest coming on Wednesday. My cousin—"

"Yoshito?" said McGurk.

"Yes. And with my two brothers and another cousin and my father, there will be people all over the house."

Mari looked so crestfallen that even McGurk was sympathetic.

"Maybe you can team up with Officer Grieg," he suggested.

"Sure," said Wanda. "Ours will be a joint entry, Mari. I've already had a wonderful idea."

"It won't beat mine," said McGurk.

"Why? Where will you be hiding Dwight?" I asked.

"Inside the monster, of course," he said. "Where else?"

His look of triumph was *obnoxious*. I mean, wasn't that just like the guy? He sets up a contest like this when he already has a perfect ready-made hiding place. Ready-made by the rest of us!

But for once Wanda didn't look indignant.

"One last question, McGurk," she said. "I take it you have no objection to the vital witness being a woman?"

"No," he said. "Just so long as she's life-size and obeys the rest of the rules." He stood up. "So that settles it, men. I'll give you until tomorrow noon to get your dummies ready. Then I'll come around and inspect them, *plus* the places you're going to conceal them in. Then, if everything's okay according to the rules, the contest can begin. The one whose vital witness is the last to be spotted by anyone who isn't a member of the Organization—that person is the winner."

"That person or *persons*, McGurk," said Wanda, giving Mari a nudge.

"Whatever," said McGurk. "Now get to work."

4 Dummies in Hiding

Well, there's no accounting for the different ways people tackle assignments like this. I mean, for starters, some people have it made. Like McGurk, with the monster in his garage. And Brains. He had several things going for him. Like:

1. Having the trapdoor to the loft in his room.

2. Having a ready-made dummy—a Red Cross inflatable person for practicing mouth-to-mouth resuscitation on. All he had to do was dress it in old clothes.

"Do your mother and father use the loft much?" McGurk asked hopefully.

"Very rarely," said Brains, looking *extremely* pleased with himself.

"Huh! Well, make sure you *feed* him properly then," said McGurk. "With decent meals. Meals you have to sneak out of the kitchen."

"No problem," said Brains, still looking smug.

I guess I myself came into the have-it-made category, with a walk-in clothes closet in my room.

"Plenty of space for him in there," I said. "Even though I didn't try to cheat on his size."

"You can say that again!" murmured McGurk.

My dummy was bigger than his. I'd used an old one-piece exercise suit of my mom's. It was made of stretch material and it swallowed up the pillows and cushions I stuffed it with. It ended up so fat I had quite a task getting some old clothes of my father's to fit. The burst soccer ball stuffed with paper that I used for its head seemed hardly big enough, even with the Chinese devil mask.

"What is he? Some kind of sumo wrestler?" asked McGurk. "And how about his air in there?"

"Louvered doors," I said, running my finger down the slats. "A nuisance, really. Moths can get in. But if moths can get in, so can air."

Willie maybe had it the easiest of all. The old shed at the end of his yard was very seldom used—the Sandowsky family not being keen gardeners. In fact, it had already proved successful as a hideout for a client—in the Case of the Condemned Cat. True, Whiskers Williams, wrongly accused of murdering some doves, wasn't very big, even for a cat. But Willie's dummy was a very skinny specimen made out of some long johns of his own that he'd outgrown, *very* lightly stuffed.

In fact, Oswald, as he called it, looked rather like Willie himself about three years ago, in his own cast-off striped jersey and narrow jeans. The melon *he'd* used for a head was bigger than McGurk's, and it made the thin creature floppily seated at a small collapsible picnic table look kind of top-heavy, especially with the large carnival mask he'd fastened onto it.

And what a mask!

I had to turn away to hide my grin. Willie had chosen a Pinocchio mask with a nose even longer than his own!

"How about toilet arrangements," said McGurk, "this far from the house?"

"Bucket," said Willie, going into a corner and kicking something that rattled.

"And food?" said McGurk.

"So long as I get to eat it myself after I've brung it," said Willie, "he won't starve."

"Fair enough," said McGurk, knowing Willie's appetite.

But while there are some people who have it made, there are others who seem to need to make it as tough as they can on themselves. I mean they just have to do it in the fanciest, most elaborate way possible.

Wanda and Mari come into this category.

Even McGurk had to hand it to them, when they introduced their dummy in the Griegs' garage.

"Wow!" he gasped. "Where did you—how did you—wow!"

It isn't often *he's* lost for words.

I mean—well—there she was, perched on a workbench, looking like a million dollars.

"Meet Meryl," said Wanda, proudly. "She witnessed a gangland killing. She's a nightclub hostess."

Meryl looked it, too!

They'd used a dressmaker's dummy for the torso and one of those plastic heads ladies keep their wigs on. This one came complete with wig—long, curly black hair—and they'd even made up the bare white face with lipstick and eye shadow and false lashes. And they'd dressed her in an old red evening gown of Mrs. Grieg's.

"We could have cheated and chosen her an ordinary full-length gown so we wouldn't have to bother much about the legs," said Wanda.

"But we didn't cheat," said Mari.

I'll say they didn't! It was one of those gowns with a long slit down one side, and Meryl was showing plenty of leg right enough!

"After all, she *is* a nightclub hostess," said Wanda.

"She sure is!" murmured Brains.

The girls must have spent hours stuffing the panty hose with shredded foam and cotton and whatnot to get the legs looking that smooth and well shaped.

And they'd topped it all off—well, *bottomed* it all off—with a pair of Wanda's mother's high-heeled black evening pumps.

"Where're you hiding her?" said McGurk. "In *here*?"

"Are you kidding?" said Wanda. She very carefully lifted Meryl from the bench and walked her to the door. "*That's* where she'll be hiding," she said. "Up there. Naturally."

And indeed, where else *would* Wanda, our expert tree-climber, have thought of but the tree house of hers, thirty feet up the sycamore and almost obscured by leaves?

"How does she get up there?" said McGurk.

"Easy," said Wanda, leading the way with Meryl bobbing at her side. "We've lowered the rope ladder, okay? If she were real she could use that. As it is, I carry her up over my shoulder. Like this."

We watched as Wanda climbed the ladder up into the leaves, with Meryl becoming a flicker of reds and blacks, as if the tree was full of cardinals.

Then the witness was hauled into the rough wooden structure out of sight, and Wanda's voice came down:

"Of course, now she's up, she stays up. Before Mom gets back from the supermarket. And"—the ladder itself began to slither up, out of sight—"I pull this up and *it* stays up, too. There won't be anyone stumbling in on Meryl in a hurry."

DUMMIES IN HIDING / 37

"Yes, but—" McGurk began.

"*I* don't need to use it," said Wanda, already clambering down the hard way.

"No," said McGurk. "But how about when you're taking her her meals?"

"No problem," said Wanda. "*I* go up first and let down a picnic box on a rope. Mari puts the food in the box and I haul it up."

"We have it all arranged, Chief McGurk," said Mari.

McGurk began to get picky.

"All arranged, huh?" he said. "So I suppose you have a bucket up there already?"

"Bucket-schmucket!" said Wanda. "Meryl has a light-weight portable toilet. The first thing we installed."

"It weighs only eight pounds," said Mari. "A Sears Pak-a-Potti. We borrowed it from my brothers' camper."

"Plus fresh water, cologne, tissues, cleansing cream," said Wanda. "Everything a woman like her might need."

McGurk no longer looked critical. His eyes were shining with real admiration.

"You've done good, Officers Grieg and Yoshimura. Someone could hide out *weeks* up there!"

"So long as the weather doesn't get rough," said Brains, looking much less sure of his own chances now.

At two o'clock that afternoon, back at HQ, after making us all take an oath on our ID cards, promising to abide

by the rules, McGurk declared the contest open.
He'd already had me type up a results table:

VITAL WITNESS PROTECTION EXERCISE			
Officer	Witness	Location	Length of time before discovery
McGurk	Dwight	Inside monster	
Rockaway	Fatso Sumo	Inside clothes closet	
Grieg & Yoshimura	Meryl	Tree house	
Sandowsky	Oswald	Garden shed	
Bellingham	John Doe	Loft space	

"*Now* we'll see who can keep their witness secret the longest," he said.

5 Two Down, Three to Go

Poor Brains!

I felt sorry for him.

At 11:45 that night (Monday), about one hour after his parents had gone to bed, he crept down to the kitchen and made up a tray for his dummy's late supper: some cold cuts and a large glass of iced tea.

Well, he got it up to his bedroom all right, without making any sound. He lowered the steps to the loft, also without making a sound. And he got the tray up into the loft without any problem. ("I didn't spill one single lousy drop of the tea," he said.)

But:

The light up there was only a dim forty-watt bulb.

And, like most lofts, the Bellinghams' was rather over-crowded with junk.

Plus the floor was only partly boarded, and he'd placed

his dummy well out of sight behind a pile of old dining chairs.

Nothing wrong with that, you might say.

Well, no. But where he'd laid the dummy down was perilously close to where the boarded area ended and the bare rafters began.

"I—I don't know *exactly* what happened," he stammered out at last, when making his report. "But I kind of stumbled and—and my right foot came down hard between the rafters—and—well—it went through the ceiling below!"

The result was that at the hour of 12:00 precisely, his father, just sinking deep into his first sleep, got a shower of shattered plaster on his head—followed immediately by what must have seemed like a Niagara of ice-cold tea.

And that was how Brains's witness was discovered after a mere ten hours.

I felt even sorrier for Wanda and Mari. In Brains's case it had been partly his own fault. He shouldn't have placed his dummy so near the danger area. But in their case it was sheer rotten bad luck.

"My guess is that a squirrel probably caused it," said Wanda, late on Tuesday afternoon, explaining what had happened earlier, at 3:20.

"How?" asked McGurk.

"Well, I'd left Meryl sitting comfortably, with her

knees up, gazing out at the treetops. And an animal or bird *must* have brushed into her right leg."

"We had stuffed it so well with foam clippings," said Mari, "that it was springy. So that when it was disturbed by the creature, her leg sprang straight out of the doorway in front of her. With its shoe still on."

"I mean about ten inches of leg is all!" said Wanda, looking bitter. "Thirty feet up! Among all the leaves and twigs!"

"So?" said McGurk.

"So that's when Ed came home," said Wanda, her shoulders slumping.

Ed is her brother. Seventeen. Grieg the Great, some kids call him (including himself). The Arnold Schwarzenegger of the senior high, say others. The best athlete in the school.

Wanda often calls him something different. She did so now.

"My brother the jerk!" she said. "The all-American, world-class, undisputed Number One Jerk! I mean, normally he wouldn't see *anything* in *any* tree. If a turkey vulture lit down on a rosebush three feet in front of his nose, he'd never notice it. But anything to do with girls"—Wanda sighed heavily. "He spotted that leg, all right!"

" *'Hey, who's that up there?'* " said Mari, imitating

Ed's deep voice. "That is what Ed said to us."

"And we just didn't know *what* to say!" groaned Wanda.

"So, go on," said McGurk. "What happened next?"

"What happened next is he suddenly thought he knew who it was," said Wanda. "He's such a rotten chauvinist. He thinks every female senior is crazy about him. So the big-headed ape decided that this one *had* to be Jody Delano—his Groupie of the Week."

" *'Okay, Jody! I can see you!'* " Mari was doing her Ed imitation again. " *'Come on down! . . . Playing hard to get, huh? Okay, girl! I'm coming to get you!'* "

"And he did," said Wanda. "Ed's a good climber, too. He swarmed up there, yodeling like Tarzan."

" *'Me Tarzan, you Jane!'* he kept saying," added Mari.

"And—and when he reached the tree house and found who—what—it really was, he got mad," said Wanda. "I mean, there was dead silence for about thirty seconds."

"Then he yelled out"—Mari looked rather pained—"something very rude. He yelled, *'I suppose you think this is funny, you obnoxious little creeps! Well here—now the joke's on you!'* "

"That's when he hurled Meryl down," said Wanda.

"Only just missing us," said Mari.

For a couple of seconds, McGurk looked genuinely sympathetic. Then he perked up.

"Officers Grieg and Yoshimura, twenty-five hours and thirty minutes," he murmured, entering it in the table.

VITAL WITNESS PROTECTION EXERCISE			
Officer	Witness	Location	Length of time before discovery
McGurk	Dwight	Inside monster	
Rockaway	Fatso Sumo	Inside clothes closet	
Grieg & Yoshimura	Meryl	Tree house	25 hrs. 30 mins.
Sandowsky	Oswald	Garden shed	
Bellingham	John Doe	Loft space	10 hrs. 0 mins.

A slight grin crossed his face as he put down his pen.

"I guess that just leaves us three, Officer Sandowsky, Officer Rockaway. I wonder who'll be next?"

You could tell it never crossed his mind that it might be *him!*

⑥ The Weeping Dummy

But it *was* McGurk's turn next, and we all got to witness it.

It happened around 9:30 the following morning, Wednesday. We'd just met up in McGurk's basement. Brains had been moaning about how much money he was going to have stopped from his allowance to help pay for the ceiling repairs. Wanda had been beefing about the cost of mending Meryl's damaged wig and shoes that *she* was going to have to pay for.

McGurk had just turned his attention to me and Willie, questioning us closely about whether we were sticking to the rules properly. I think he hoped to disqualify us on a technicality. Something that would leave him the undisputed winner.

"You know you have to act like Oswald's bucket has been *used*, don't you?" he said to Willie.

"Huh?" grunted Willie. "Sorry, McGurk. What did you say?"

"I *thought* you weren't listening, Officer Sandowsky! What's with you?"

Willie had been sitting with his eyes closed and his head in the air. His nostrils were twitching like mad.

"That melon you used for Dwight's head," he murmured. "Getting kind of overripe, isn't it? It must be stinking the garage out."

A general murmur arose. It hadn't taken Willie's supersensitive nose to sniff that something had gone bad. I'd caught more than a whiff of it myself. So had the others. The only difference was that we hadn't been able to identify it.

"So *that's* what it is!" said Wanda.

"I thought it was a garbage bag that had burst open," said Brains.

"Don't worry," said McGurk. "I noticed it, too. Just before you all got here. When I brought Dwight into the house to take him to the toilet. Mom had gone out to the store. I'll fix him a new head while I'm about it, I thought." He grinned. "But it isn't as bad as all *that*, Officer Sandowsky. It isn't wafting all the way across from the garage. It's only in the next room."

I pounced. I'd sensed some infringement of the rules.

"Oh, yes, McGurk? So what's he doing *there*? Why isn't he back inside the monster?"

"Not so fast, Officer Rockaway," he said. "It's only a temporary emergency move. Because while I was in the bathroom with him I heard Mom's car come back. So I stashed him down here until she'd finished unloading the groceries."

"So why is he still here?" asked Brains.

"Because then *you* all started arriving. I want to make sure Mom's out of the way before I risk giving him a new head and taking him back." He glared around. "Hey, what *is* this? I'm only being careful. If some of *you* jerks had been more careful you'd still be in with a chance!"

"It makes sense, I guess," I said.

"You bet it makes sense!" said McGurk. "I mean it isn't as if he's been discovered—"

He broke off.

The ear-splitting scream seemed to have come from inside that very room.

"Next door!" gasped McGurk.

"It sounded like your mother!" said Wanda.

And she was right.

When we all rushed into the game room, we found Mrs. McGurk flopped in the old leather armchair, staring across the Ping-Pong table with a look of utter horror.

She was clutching a table-tennis paddle as if it had been the first weapon to come to hand—though how she hoped *that* would have defended her, I don't know.

Because what had given her such a fright made even some of *us* turn pale, and *we'd* had a rough idea what to expect.

But Dwight really did look sinister up there, lying stretched out across the top of a cupboard, with one boxing-gloved arm dangling over the side like he was holding a club, and his gorilla face leering down at the poor lady.

The weirdest thing, though, was the tears. The great oozy, oily tears slowly falling from the mask's eyeholes. *I* realized at once that the overripe melon inside must have split, but I bet Mrs. McGurk *still* has nightmares about it!

Anyway, she is one real good sport, and she was soon laughing about it.

"When I first caught the smell I thought it was a cat," she said. "Maybe a stray cat had wandered in and gotten shut in one of the rooms down here. Then when I heard you all talking in this one, I knew it had to be the game room. So that's where I decided to investigate first. . . ."

I quote that because it shows where McGurk gets most of his detective instinct from. I only wish he'd inherited her sporting spirit along with it!

Because, whatever else he may be, McGurk is definitely *not* a good loser!

"If you jerks hadn't come when you did, I'd probably have managed to return Dwight to his proper hiding place in good time!" he growled, as he entered the figures next to his own name: *43 hours, 31 minutes.*

7 The Prowling Dummy

But when it comes to excuses, it was I who had the best.

I mean, how was I to know that Cousin Benny would be staying the night? His own father didn't know until late that afternoon. Aunt Lorna wasn't supposed to be having the new baby for another four weeks.

Anyway, she had to be rushed to the hospital, with my uncle accompanying her to be present at the birth, and Benny was dumped on us.

Now Benny is bad news.

He's only seven and he's not very big, but being not very big only helps him to shove his nose into everything and every place. Aunt Lorna and Uncle Ethan say it's because he's hyperactive. *I* say that it's because Cousin Benny has been spoiled rotten and is one bratty kid.

So you can imagine my alarm. When Cousin Benny comes to stay the night—like the time they first moved into the neighborhood—guess whose bedroom they put him in?

You've got it.

I didn't get a single wink of sleep that first time, because although Benny did drop off the minute he hit the sack, he was just as hyperactive asleep. Tossing, turning, twitching, rearing up, flopping down, singing—yes, *singing!*—and even asking his dumb questions in his sleep. Since then, I've always insisted he sleep in a spare bed at the other end of the room. (And he *still* keeps me awake half the night!)

The problem this time, of course, was that there seemed to be no way of keeping him from stumbling across Fatso Sumo. The fact that the dummy was stashed away in *my* private clothes closet? Hah! Closed doors are a *challenge* to Benny.

In fact, there was only one thing I could do. That was to move Fatso to a place where I could hope to keep him out of Benny's reach. After all, this was permitted under the rules. Hadn't McGurk himself spoken about "a temporary emergency move" in connection with Dwight?

It didn't take me long to think of a perfect hiding place. The only trouble was that the move would have to be made after dark. But even this didn't create too much of a problem. All Benny wanted to do while it was still light was race around the backyard on my bicycle, with me holding onto him to keep him from wrecking it totally. And then fly my kite and all three of my model airplanes until he'd gotten the kite tangled up in a tree and two of the planes stranded on next-door's roof.

By the time Mom called us in for dinner, he was all set to go hunting down the neighborhood cats with a fishing net he'd found in the garage. Then, after dinner, where he sampled everything in sight and finished nothing, he insisted on watching TV. This meant trying out every channel until he found something that suited him—a western where a whole bunch of grown-up Bennies were committing mayhem on each other with guns, knives, ropes, and sticks of dynamite.

Which is when I snuck upstairs and rescued Fatso Sumo.

It was dark outside by now. The hiding place I'd thought of was the flat roof of the garage, just under my room window. The streetlights were on, but it was shadowy down there, close against the wall. And since there was nobody out in the street just then, it was a cinch for me to slide open the window quietly and then casually lower Fatso like it was a sleeping bag I was putting out to air off.

So it was with a great sense of satisfaction that I turned out the light an hour later and said good-night to Benny. That was, of course, after he'd jumped up and down a few thousand times on his bed, using it as a trampoline. And what *especially* gave me that sense of satisfaction was that the little jerk had proved me right. One of the first things he'd done on entering the room had been to open the closet doors and swing on the spare hangers. Fatso wouldn't have stood a chance!

But Fatso was safe. Even Benny hadn't thought of leaning out of the window. (If he had, I was all set to make a safety issue of it and bar his way and yell for Dad to come and restrain him for his own good.) So Fatso remained serene and undiscovered, stretched out in the shadows, enjoying the warm evening air and the song of the cicadas and . . . off I went to sleep. I guess I must have been worn out.

That was why it was all the more of a shock when, some time later, I heard a giant's voice hollering, *"All right, you! Come on down offa there! Right now! This is the police!"*

I opened my eyes and immediately shut them again, dazzled by the light that was flooding in at the window. I felt something hard stomp on my chest and wriggle about, then realized it was Benny when he said, "It's the cops! They're shining a light up *here!*"

And so they were.

It was Patrolman Cassidy doing the talking, with the car all lit up behind him. Lights were going on in other windows, too. Right next to mine, I heard my parents' window slide up and my father say, "What is it, Officer?"

"No problem, sir," said Mr. Cassidy. "Just a prowler. We've had several complaints from all over the neighborhood and now we've found him. *All right, you! Come on down!*"

I sighed. I heaved Benny off my legs—where he was now kneeling, shouting, "Shoot him, Mr. Cassidy! Why don't you shoot him?" I switched on the bedside lamp. I noted the time (11:15). Then I lifted the bottom half of the window and said, "It's okay, Mr. Cassidy. It's only a dummy. I can explain everything. . . ."

8 Willie's Bombshell

When I arrived at our headquarters the next morning, my mood was definitely not good.

I mean, for one thing, there had been the bawling-out I'd had from my father in his den. Before breakfast, too.

As if this wasn't bad enough, the news came through that Aunt Lorna had delivered a baby boy, a little underweight but fine and healthy. I'd been hoping it would be a girl. The thought of another guy like Benny coming into the world ready to step into his brother's shoes was hard to take. Especially on that of all mornings.

And then there were his parting words, just before driving off with my mother to see the new baby.

"Hey, Joey! I've been thinking. You aren't all *that* smart, are you?"

"What do you mean?" I asked.

"Trying to hide the dummy out *there*. It was stupid! *I'd* have hid him in the clothes closet!"

I was still feeling sore when I entered McGurk's basement. To give you an idea of just how sore, here's a copy
of the note I'd made plus the doodling I'd done all around
it in the meantime:

Fatso Sumo
discovered 11:15 p.m.
Wednesday June 24

Funnily enough, the others weren't looking any too
cheerful either.

"You're late," grumbled McGurk.

"Yeah," was all I said to that.

"Have you seen anything of Officer Sandowsky?" he
asked.

"Yeah," I said. "He was just going on an errand. Says
he won't be long."

"Huh!" grunted McGurk. "So what are *you* looking so miserable about?"

I took a deep breath and told him.

For a few minutes they perked up. Some of them even laughed. Anyone would think there'd been something *funny* about last night's fiasco. Even Mari, who'd been looking the most troubled of all, gave a wan smile.

"Your vital witness exercise seems to be causing mayhem all over the place, McGurk," said Wanda.

He was entering my score: *57 hours, 15 minutes.*

"Yeah, well," he murmured, "you can't make an omelette without breaking eggs. And this exercise could come in very useful one day."

"Anyway," said Brains, "it looks like Willie's the winner. Trust *him* for sheer dumb luck!"

"We don't know that," said McGurk, putting the pen down. "We haven't had his report yet. Maybe Patrolman Cassidy saw *his* dummy last night, too. When he was searching for the prowler. Maybe he took a peek in Willie's shed and discovered Oswald *before* he spotted Fatso."

I sighed. "No. When I met Willie going on his errand he asked me what all the ruckus was about last night. And when I told him he said it was tough, but that made him the winner."

"Hm!" murmured McGurk. "We'll check anyway." He

turned to Mari. "Now, Officer Yoshimura. You were saying? Before Officer Rockaway arrived. About your cousin Yoshito."

"Yes, Chief McGurk." She was looking very troubled again. "He was due to arrive last night. In time for supper. And to stay as our guest until Sunday."

"But he's been delayed, right?"

"Yes. He called. Long after we expected him. He told my father there had been an unforeseen delay."

"And he didn't say why, huh?"

McGurk's eyes had narrowed, but he didn't look all that bothered.

"No," said Mari. "My father said it sounded like a pay phone and they got cut off. So maybe he was going to explain but did not have the time."

McGurk shrugged. "Well, it happens," he said.

"I know!" said Mari. "But it is so *unlike* Yoshito. He is always very polite. We expected he would find another telephone. But we have not heard from him since."

"Go on," murmured McGurk, his eyes narrowing again. His suspicions are always aroused when he hears about somebody not acting in their usual way. "Anything else?"

"My father says he sounded out of breath," said Mari. "And—well, maybe he is sick."

"Well, let's hope he gets better by Saturday," said

Wanda. "It won't be much of a success without him."

"Oh, I don't know," said McGurk. "There'll be our monster in the parade and—"

That was when Willie burst in. He didn't look much like a winner now.

"McGurk! Guys! I—I—"

He tottered across to his chair, eyes rolling with a mixture of awe and horror.

"Come on, Officer Sandowsky!" said McGurk, sternly. "Take a deep breath and tell us what's eating you."

"*Me?*" cried Willie. "Eating *me?* It isn't what's eating *me,* McGurk! It's what—who—what's been eating—" He shuddered. "Oh, gosh!" he groaned, closing his eyes.

"Officer Sandowsky! Pull yourself together, man! What's happened?"

"S-s-something terrible!"

"*What?*"

"Os-os-os-"

"Oswald?"

"Yeah! My dummy! It—he—I just can't believe it!"

"Go *on,* Officer Sandowsky! Are you trying to tell us Patrolman Cassidy *did* discover him, after all?"

"P-patrolman Cassidy?"

"Yes. Last night. When he—"

"No. No. Oswald was okay this morning when I took him his breakfast."

"So?"

"So when I went back to him just now—ten, fifteen minutes later—he—he'd—"

"Yes?"

"He'd *ate* it!"

We all stared. Even McGurk looked stunned.

"Let's get this straight," he said. "*Oswald* had eaten it?"

"Yeah—he must have."

"Oswald the *dummy* had eaten the breakfast?"

"Every scrap," said Willie. "Two eggs over easy, three rashers of Canadian bacon, *everything*. I'd left it under one of those tin things to keep hot. I was gonna eat it myself. Then I heard Mom call out. She wanted me to get some coffee from the deli. So I did. And when I got back—"

He closed his eyes, with a look of total perplexity on his face—probably going over the scene again in his head.

"When you got back, Officer Sandowsky?" McGurk gently prompted him. "The breakfast had been *eaten*?"

"Yes. Every—every scrap!"

"Could it have been your mom?" I asked. "Playing tricks?"

Willie shook his head.

"No. No way. She doesn't fool around like that. Anyway, she was taking a bath. She'd called out to me from the bathroom window. And she was still in there when I got back with the coffee."

"Could it have been rats?" Wanda asked.

Willie glared at her.

"We don't have rats!" he said. "I'd have smelled 'em long ago if we did. And rats who've learned to use knives and forks? And to leave them neatly in line on the plate when they're through? Huh! Some *rats*!"

That silenced us.

"Also rats who use after-shave?" he said suddenly.

McGurk looked up.

"After-shave?"

"Yeah," said Willie. "Brute Force Twelve brand."

"But—"

"And I'm not through yet!" Willie glared at Wanda again. "And rats who switch a dummy's clothes for their own? Huh? How about *that*, ma'am?" He turned back to McGurk. "Because that's what happened. They took my old striped jersey off of him and put a windbreaker in its place!"

"So this had to be a *person*—a person or persons unknown," said McGurk, slowly getting up from his chair.

"That's what I'm trying to tell you," said Willie, seeming to forget he'd been blaming Oswald himself up until now. "I mean, rats, yes." He gave Wanda an apologetic glance. "Maybe if I *had* caught a whiff of them—and it had just been Oswald's *head.*"

"What about Oswald's head?" said McGurk.

Willie groaned.

"That's the first thing I saw! Whoever did it—he—she—they—"

He broke off, shuddering again.

"What, Officer Sandowsky? Spit it out! They *what?*"

"They ate Oswald's head as well!"

McGurk made for the door. His eyes were gleaming. His hair seemed to have caught fire.

"Come on, men! It looks like we have a case at last!"

⑨ The Scene of the Crime

Willie's shed is tucked away among the bushes at the end of the backyard. This morning, despite the bright sunshine, it somehow looked menacing.

"Approach with caution, men," said McGurk. "The perpetrator may have come back to the scene of the crime."

Gently, he pressed his ear to the closed door, his freckles all bunched together in a fierce frown.

I found myself holding my breath. Willie's breath was coming out in quick, nervous little rasps. He was standing sideways, ready to run. Brains was behind me. Wanda and Mari were standing a little apart. Wanda had a hand on Mari's shoulder, whether to comfort herself or Mari, I don't know.

Then, when McGurk took out a handkerchief and placed it on the handle of the door, Wanda seemed to come out of her trance.

"Oh, for heaven's sake, McGurk! What's with the fingerprint routine? This isn't a *murder* case!"

"We don't know that!" muttered McGurk.

But the scornful comment must have embarrassed him some, because then he did open the door.

Still gingerly, though. Without stepping inside.

We moved closer behind him and stood there gazing at the interior.

It was fairly dim. There were some old dark-green curtains at the window. Willie had drawn them shut the day he'd put Oswald in there. McGurk had even praised him for this: "Good thinking, Officer Sandowsky. It wouldn't be much use to your vital witness if *anyone* could peek in and see him."

But there was light enough to see what had given Willie such a scare.

Because it really did look like the scene of a crime. McGurk had me make out a careful plan of it later, and here it is:

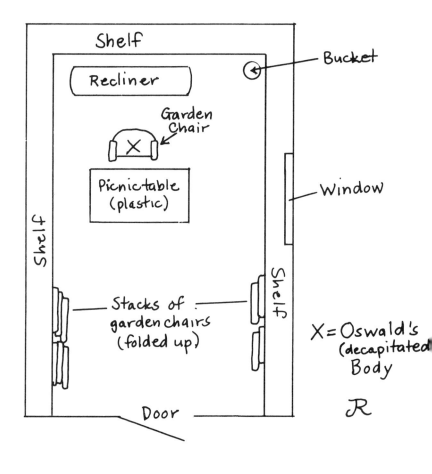

Naturally, it didn't look as tidy as that. The waist-high shelves were cluttered up with junk: stacks of plant pots, piles of yellowing newspapers, burlap sacking, old coffee jars with rusty nails in them, and so on. There were also spades and garden forks and rakes and things, leaning in the corners. Cobwebby jerry cans and sacks of bulb fiber and dusty cardboard boxes filled the spaces under the shelves.

But right then, as we stood with McGurk at the threshold, all we had eyes for was the victim. Yes, victim. That was what McGurk was calling him now.

And, sure enough, victim is what Oswald did look like, slumped there at the table, facing us. The victim of a horrible, brutal murder, with most of his head missing. Only the Pinocchio mask remained, hanging by its string from the cane on which the melon had been stuck. There was something incredibly sad about the way that empty face was tilted forward, with its long nose resting on the plate.

"Be careful not to touch anything, men," said McGurk, as we slowly stepped forward.

The plate looked like it might have been licked, it was so clean. And, laid across it, perfectly in line, were the knife and fork—just as Willie had described them.

At the side of the plate, in a tidy heap, were fragments of the victim's skull—yellow pieces of melon rind, some large, some small, all gnawed bare of any flesh.

Being the same shade of yellow, the windbreaker was what caught my eye next. Whoever had swiped the striped jersey hadn't put Oswald's arms in the sleeves. The yellow garment was simply draped over the shoulders of the stuffed long johns, with the reputedly leather sleeves dangling loose. (I say *reputedly* leather because the material was so fine and flexible it looked at first like silk.) Anyway, worn like that, it gave the remains of

Oswald a rakish, swaggering look that I found a trifle creepy.

It wasn't half so creepy, though, as what had caught McGurk's eye.

"Is—is this the dish-cover you mentioned, Officer Sandowsky?" he asked.

"Yes."

"Was it like this when you found it?"

"Yes."

I'd missed it myself because it hadn't been *on* the table, but suspended a few feet above it. It was tied to the pull-string of the light switch. McGurk pulled the string and the light went on. The dish-cover was now gently swaying. It looked so weird that I made a rough sketch of it right then. This:

Dish-cover found dangling at the Scene of the Crime
June 25 A. M.

"There are some smears of yellow on it," McGurk murmured, peering closer.

"Egg?" said Brains.

"Yes," said Willie, giving it a sniff. "Must have come off his breakfast. The plate *was* kinda piled high when I put the cover on."

"But this is on the *outside* of the cover," said McGurk.

Willie shrugged.

"Well, off of his fingers then."

"He doesn't look like such a messy eater to me," said McGurk, glancing at the neat lineup of utensils. He turned back to the dangling dish-cover. "But why hang it up like that?"

"Some kind of a prank?" suggested Wanda.

McGurk didn't reply. He was bending even closer to the cover, squinting at the yellow marks.

I thought he was overdramatizing, as usual. Brains must have thought so, too. He turned to Willie.

"Do you usually bring him—Oswald—hot food?" he asked.

"No," said Willie. "Not always. But this morning, knowing Mom would be in the bathroom for hours— well, at least *one* hour—she always is—I took the opportunity to cook the kid a proper breakfast."

"On second thought, not so much *smears*," McGurk was murmuring, "but more like flakes and—and *spatters* of egg. . . ."

No one was taking much notice of him now.

"I wonder if Sandra Ennis or some of those other jerks got wind of the exercise?" said Wanda. "And decided to pull a prank?"

"A very *expensive* prank," said Mari. Obedient to McGurk, she hadn't directly touched anything, but, with an old flower stick that she'd picked up from the shelf, she had gently poked open wider the front of the windbreaker and was examining the label. I made a sketch of *that*, too:

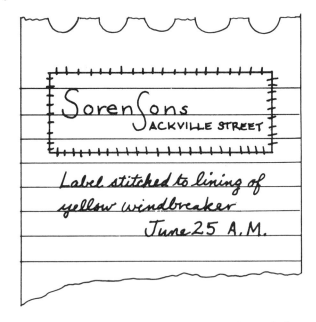

"That is a London store," said Mari. "My father often buys clothes there when he goes to England. This windbreaker would have cost *hundreds* of dollars."

"Pounds," said Brains. "In England it would have been pounds sterling, not dollars."

"It would be *that* expensive, Officer Yoshimura?" said McGurk, looking interested.

"Yes, Chief McGurk. *Very* expensive. In dollars *or* pounds."

"Hmm!" murmured McGurk. "It's most likely a kid's, too. Same size as Oswald, by the look of it."

"Well, I wouldn't say that, McGurk," said Wanda. "If you imagine it with the arms in the sleeves they'd be kind of long. A teenager's, maybe. Or a small man's."

"But why?" I said. "Why would anyone want to switch clothes? I mean, just eating the food was enough, surely?"

There was a rattle. McGurk was inspecting the bucket.

"They didn't use *that*, anyway," he said. Then he came back to the table. "Officer Rockaway, did you say Patrolman Cassidy mentioned something about a prowler in the neighborhood last night?"

"Yes," I said. "Obviously someone had mistaken Fatso Sumo for one."

McGurk shook his head firmly.

"No. That wasn't the way you told it to us. Come on. Think. What *exactly* did he say?"

"Uh—'We—we've had complaints'—uh—'several complaints'—"

"Yeah. Go on!"

McGurk's eyes were gleaming.

"Why, yes!" I said, " 'several complaints *from all over the neighborhood*'!"

"That's what I thought you'd said." McGurk switched off the light.

"You think—?" Brains began.

"That this is the work of a real prowler—yeah," said McGurk. "It has to be. And maybe a dangerous prowler, too. Come on, men. Let's see if we can find out more about him!"

"Where from?" asked Wanda.

"Straight from the horse's mouth," said McGurk. "Where else?"

10 The Monster Comes to Life?

I don't know how Patrolman Cassidy would have liked being called a horse. But I do know how he liked being visited by a bunch of kids at his home.

Answer: *Not—one—little—bit!*

Mrs. Cassidy must have been out, because he had to answer the doorbell himself.

In his bathrobe. With half his face covered in shaving foam. His gray moustache stuck out bristlier than ever.

"Oh, it's *you* again, is it?" he said, giving me a sour look.

"You can't blame Officer Rockaway for last night, sir," said McGurk. "He was only carrying out my orders. A very important training exercise. And it looks like it might turn out to be a big help to *you*."

Mr. Cassidy's eyes narrowed.

"Oh, really, M'Turk?"

I breathed a little easier. Mr. Cassidy is really quite friendly toward the Organization. Stern, but friendly.

And this business of pretending to get McGurk's name wrong is one of his little jokes.

"That's Mc*Gurk*, sir," said our leader.

"Sure, McKirk. So what's all this about being a big help to *me*?"

"In your assignment, sir. Tracking down the prowler."

Mr. Cassidy looked blank.

"What prowler?"

"The one you thought Fatso was. Last night, sir."

"Fatso?"

"The dummy, sir."

Mr. Cassidy frowned, beginning to look mad at me again.

"Oh, *him*? Yeah. So?"

"Have you apprehended him yet, sir?" said McGurk. "The *real* prowler?"

Mr. Cassidy sighed, took the towel from his neck, and wiped off the remains of the foam.

"Not unless he's been caught since I came off duty. Why?"

"Well, we might be able to help," said McGurk. "Can you give us his description?"

Mr. Cassidy shook his head.

"No. The reports were very sketchy. Why? Have *you* spotted a prowler?"

"Well, not really," said McGurk. "Uh—he wasn't a *wanted* person, was he? Someone on the run?"

Mr. Cassidy's moustache twitched.

"The trouble with *you*, M'Quirk, is your imagination. Too vivid. Nah! Prowlers are usually just creeps, snoopers, Peeping Toms. *Possibly* would-be burglars, casing some house or other. But nine times out of ten, just plain nuisances."

McGurk was looking very disappointed.

"Anyway," said Patrolman Cassidy, "whatever they're doing their prowling *for*, you leave that kind of thing to *us*. Okay?"

"Oh, yes, sir! Of course, Mr. Cassidy!" said McGurk, getting ready to go. "It's just that we'll keep our eyes peeled and let you know of anything suspicious."

"You do that, McGurk," said the cop. "Hey—and make your report to the duty officer at the station, huh? Not to a guy who's trying to get some well-earned rest between shifts!"

Back on the street, Willie turned to McGurk.

"Shouldn't you have told him about Oswald's breakfast, McGurk?"

"I was going to," said our leader. "But when he made that crack about my imagination, I thought why bother!"

Brains nodded.

"But that *is* why you thought it might be a fugitive, right, McGurk? The breakfast being wolfed like that?"

"Yeah," said McGurk. "Plus why else would anyone switch clothes with a dummy?"

"Oh, come on, McGurk!" said Wanda. "It could have been just some poor starving homeless person."

McGurk glared at her, scornfully.

"What? With a windbreaker he could have hocked for a hundred dollars or more? Use your head, Officer Grieg!"

After that, McGurk decided to stop by at HQ and pick up his magnifying glass.

"I want to go over the scene of the crime again. I'm still puzzled about those traces of egg. I have a hunch it could be a vital clue. It could—"

"Hush!" hissed Brains. "What—what's *that*?"

We'd reached the McGurk driveway and were just passing the open garage door. Mrs. McGurk's car was in its usual place and so, of course, was our monster.

"It seems to be coming from its insides!" whispered Brains.

The "it" he was referring to was a strange noise. I mean, it wasn't strange in itself. Merely a kind of light tap-tapping. Maybe a clock ticking. If it had been coming from under the car you might have thought it was someone doing a repair job.

But this was coming from inside the monster.

"It sounds like something's scratching around in there," said Brains.

"Have *you* got rats, McGurk?" asked Wanda, looking pale.

"Or—or *snakes?*" Willie whispered, looking even paler.

Sure enough, the sound had switched to a slow, steady, relentless hissing and swishing.

Then suddenly Mari clutched my arm. The dazzling mix of patterns had always given me the impression that the monster's skin was quivering and trembling.

But now, darn me if it wasn't *actually* doing it!

And not only quivering and trembling, but *shuddering!*

Accompanied by a new sound, a louder rumbling—a *thundering!*

"It is as if it is coming to life!" said Mari. (The thud-thud-thudding was going on as she spoke, so I knew it couldn't be one of her voice-throwing tricks this time.) "As if those are its heartbeats!"

Then Willie gave a yelp and someone else screamed and most of us turned to run, and the scuffling of our feet on the gravel drowned out every other sound.

For the monster had suddenly reared up, front legs flapping in the air.

11 The Desperate Drummer

"Wait! *Please!*"

There was something in the voice that made us all stop and turn. It wasn't very loud, but it was urgent and anxious. Friendly but—yes—*desperate*.

Its owner was just stepping out from the uptilted shell of the monster. He laid it down carefully. He was clutching a couple of dry bristly paintbrushes in one hand. I guessed they'd come from the bunch lying about on the workbench. He was only slightly built, maybe twenty years old.

"Yoshito!" gasped Mari, running up and flinging her arms around him. "My cousin!"

"My old jersey!" gasped Willie. "*Oswald's* jersey!"

It was, too. I'd have recognized those broad black horizontal stripes anywhere. The jersey looked a bit tight on the newcomer, and terribly tatty compared with his light-blue tailored jeans and the fancy cowboy boots.

"The guy who ate Oswald's breakfast!" said McGurk, as Yoshito disentangled himself from Mari.

"Yeah!" said Willie. "And ate his head for dessert!"

Yoshito Nakanishi bowed slightly.

"Yes," he said. "Alas, I am guilty." He spoke very good English—almost as good as Mari's. "But I can explain," he added, glancing anxiously beyond us, out into the street. "Can we go someplace private? Someplace *safe*? Your office, yes?"

"You'd *better* explain!" said McGurk. But his curiosity was getting the better of him, I could tell. "If you'll just follow me, sir," he said, more politely.

He led the way to the basement door, unlocked it, and invited Yoshito inside. All this time, the newcomer had been careful to put the rest of us between himself and the street, half crouching. Only when he was well inside the room did he straighten up.

"Take a seat," said McGurk, offering him the one opposite his rocking chair—Wanda's. "Officer Grieg, you go stand by the door and keep an eye on the driveway. Let us know if anyone comes." He turned to Yoshito. "Now then, sir, tell us how we may help you."

Yoshito nodded and for the first time gave us all a big smile. He seemed much more relaxed. Relaxed enough anyway to start tapping out a kind of soft-shoe shuffle rhythm on the table with the bristle ends of the brushes.

I noticed then that he had a gold bracelet watch on one of his incredibly flexible wrists.

And all the time he was making his opening statement, he kept up that fluent swishing and tapping, sometimes using the handle ends of the brushes. Even if Mari hadn't been there to identify him, I would have known we were listening to one very classy professional drummer.

Anyway, here's what he told us in those first few minutes:

Yoshito Nakanishi's Statement: Part One

"I must first apologize to *you*, Willie Sandowsky. I was desperate for someplace safe to hide and rest. After being out in the open all night, in a strange place, keeping to the shadows, lurking behind bushes. Never knowing whether some dog would give the alarm. Or if the police car that was cruising around would spot me in its light.

"After daybreak it was more difficult still. I dared not move around at all. There was a shed near the bushes I was hiding in, and I wondered whether it would be safe to spend some hours there. That is when I see you, Willie Sandowsky. Coming down and going into it, bearing tray of food. And I thought, Shoot! The shed *is* in use after all! But then I hear your mother calling out for you to run errand, and you obey like a very good son, and leave the shed and—and the tray."

Yoshito's drumming got rather frantic here.

"I hadn't realized just how ravenous I was," he said. "And the smell! So delicious! I just couldn't resist it."

"*I* can buy that!" said Willie, his stomach rumbling in sympathy. (Yoshito was now thumping the table with the heel of his hand.)

"Hey—just a minute!" said McGurk. "Were you doing this drumming while you were eating Oswald's breakfast? Did you hang up the dish-cover and tap it with the knife and fork?"

"Yes," said Yoshito, looking surprised. "I just couldn't resist that, either. I never can. I am always practicing. Always. And the more excited or worried I am, the more I do it."

"So go on," said McGurk. "Back in the hut—"

The drumming became faster and faster.

Yoshito Nakanishi's Statement (Continued)

"It didn't take me long to finish the food, you can bet. I wasn't sure how soon Willie would be back. But then I had the idea to switch my jacket for this jersey. All through the night I had been worried about how conspicuous the bright lemon color was. But, just as I was putting on the jersey, I hear Willie return and I think, Oh-oh, now I am caught!

"But first he went into house, so I slipped quietly out

of hut and into bushes. Only just in time." (He was drumming at breakneck speed now.) "Then as soon as he entered the hut I heard him say, 'Oh, no! Wait until McGurk hears about *this*!' And then I knew who he was. I *had* been wondering, on account of his long—uh—well, certain personal features. But when he mentioned McGurk, then I was sure. I remembered all the letters Mari has written to me—about your names and what you looked like—and I thought, Good. They might be just the guys to help me out!

"So I followed Willie to here—"

"Just a sec," said McGurk. "Why didn't you introduce yourself to Officer Sandowsky straight off?"

Yoshito shook his head. He made shivery noises with the brushes.

"He was still in shock. Besides, it would have been impolite not to put my request to the head of the Organization first."

That seemed to please McGurk no end.

"Quite right," he said. "Naturally. Go on, sir."

"So I followed him here. And then—keeping under cover as much as possible—I read the notice stuck on the glass panel in the door, and I think, Bingo! This is the place! But—" (The brush strokes became very whispery.) "I listen carefully. I hear voices but not what is being said. I am still not sure who is with you. Maybe a parent. I do not want to get too close and peer through the glass because I am in very great danger and dare not take too many risks.

"Anyway, before I could make sure, you all came rushing out. With you, McGurk, saying, 'Come on, we're going to investigate this right away!' Well, I knew where you meant. So I decided to lie low until you returned. I had already seen the creature of many cloths in the garage and decided it would be a good hiding place. And—well—you know the rest."

McGurk frowned.

"Some of it," he said.

"Excuse me?"

"We only know *some* of the rest, sir. You haven't told us yet what this very great danger is. And why you're so scared of being seen." McGurk leaned forward. "Seen who *by*?"

There was a pause. Yoshito quit drumming. He glanced uneasily at Wanda.

"Is everything okay out there?" he asked. "No silver-gray car on the street?"

She shook her head. "No," she said.

"Who are you so scared of, sir?" McGurk persisted.

Yoshito Nakanishi sighed. He even laid the brushes down on the table—carefully.

"The—the two men," he said. "They are in the neighborhood. I have seen their car. A silver-gray Mercedes."

"So who *are* they?" said McGurk.

Yoshito shook his head.

"I do not *know*." He cast another nervous glance at the door. "It is better that *you* do not know, either. All I need is someplace to hide from them until the gig on Saturday. The drumming exhibition."

"But why do you not come to our house, Yoshito?" said Mari. "We have been expecting—"

"No, Mari." Yoshito's tone was very firm. "No way can I do that. I must not risk making trouble for you and your family. These men *are* dangerous, I am sure."

"Well, *great!*" snapped McGurk. Then he quickly calmed down. "That's all very fine, sir," he said patiently. "But if we're gonna help you, we need to know *why*. Why you're so scared, and what you're so scared *of*." He gave Yoshito a beady look. "Hey—you're not on the run from the *law*, are you?"

"McGurk!" gasped Wanda. "This is Mari's *cousin!*"

"It's okay," said Yoshito. "It is a fair question." He turned to McGurk. "But I cannot involve you too much. All I can say is this: I am not on the run from the law. At least—"

He hesitated. McGurk pounced.

"At least what?"

"At least *they* pretend to be connected with the law. But they are phonies."

"So, for Pete's sake, *why* are you on the run from them?" said McGurk, flaring up again. "Why—?"

His mother's voice broke in. She sounded very close. "Jack! Who's in there with you?"

In a flash, the stripe-jerseyed figure at my side dove straight under the table and vanished, with only the paintbrushes on top to show he'd been there at all.

12 The Men in the Mercedes

"Only the guys, Mom. The—my officers . . ."

McGurk had bounded to the door as fast as Yoshito had gone under the table.

But he needn't have worried. Mrs. McGurk was at the top of the basement stairs.

"Is Willie there?" we heard her say.

"Yes."

"Well, tell him his mother's on the phone. She wants to know about the dirty dishes in the shed. And whose is the yellow windbreaker? She sounds worried."

"I'd better go up and tell her—uh—I—" stammered Willie.

McGurk waved him back.

"Is she still on the line, Mom?"

"Yes."

"Well, tell her we're on our way and we'll explain everything. No need to worry. Just an Organization exercise."

We heard Mrs. McGurk laugh. "Oh, *that*! Okay, I'll let her know."

When McGurk closed the door, Yoshito emerged from under the table.

"What about me?" he said. "It will be risky for me to go with you!"

"No sweat," said McGurk, locking the inner door. "You wait here. We won't be long. Mom only comes down if something unusual attracts her attention."

Yoshito still looked doubtful—a scared fugitive again, with darting, hunted eyes.

"And if it helps," said McGurk, "you can lock the outer door behind us, too. Then *no one* can drop in on you."

That seemed to relieve Yoshito.

"Why couldn't you just let Willie tell his mom on the phone?" I asked, as we hurried along the street.

"And blurt out something that might give our secret away?" said McGurk. "No. This is one of those times when *I* do the talking and everyone else keeps silent. Okay?"

Mrs. Sandowsky didn't take much convincing, as it happened.

She'd been worried, yes. She'd seen us all go into the shed but hadn't seen us leave. Then, when she'd gone down to ask Willie where he'd put the coffee, the sight of the headless dummy and the dangling dish-cover had given her a shock. Not as big a shock as Dwight had given Mrs. McGurk, but enough to arouse her parental suspicion.

Fortunately, she must have told Mrs. McGurk about Oswald's body, and Mrs. McGurk had been able to tell her about the dummy *she'd* stumbled across.

So once more McGurk had it made.

"It was a witness-hiding exercise, right?" Willie's mother said, laughing, before McGurk had even begun to explain.

"Yes, ma'am."

"But isn't that beautiful windbreaker rather too good for dummies?" asked Mrs. Sandowsky. "Whose is it?"

That one caught McGurk off guard.

"Uh—" he began. "It—uh—"

"It belongs to a member of my family, Mrs. Sandowsky," said Mari.

"Well, if I were you, Mari," said Mrs. Sandowsky, "I'd take it right back home before anyone misses it."

On the way down the Sandowsky driveway, McGurk warned Mari to fold the windbreaker inside out, with only the black silk lining showing.

"Ah, yes, of course, Chief McGurk!" she said, taking it from her left shoulder, where she'd let it swing casually. "*I* should have thought of that myself."

"What difference does it make?" said Willie.

"The color," I said. "That telltale yellow. Right, McGurk?"

"Right," said McGurk. "Didn't you hear what Yoshito said, Officer Sandowsky? You never know where those two guys might be. Some detectives *we'd* be if we led them direct to our client's hiding place!"

And, by golly, his instincts had been right! We couldn't have gone more than a dozen paces along the sidewalk before a large silver-gray Mercedes came purring past.

"Oh, no!" gasped Wanda. "Don't tell me—"

She broke off. The car had come to a sudden stop. Then it began to reverse toward us.

I glanced down uneasily at Mari, but there wasn't even the narrowest strip of yellow showing in the jacket over her arm. Just the black lining.

It *was* Mari who had caught their attention, though.

"Hey, little girl!" said the man in the passenger seat. "You're Japanese, aren't you?"

They both wore business suits. They must have had the air-conditioning on, because they both looked very cool. Their eyes were hard as they looked us up and down, even though their mouths were smiling. Cool, tough, middle-aged, heavily built. They *could* have been cops, I guessed.

"I was born in Japan, yes," said Mari, politely.

The passenger turned to the driver.

"You know what, Roy?" he drawled.

"What's that, Stan?"

"I bet you she's called Nakanishi. Right, little girl?"

Mari didn't even blink at the mention of our client's name. McGurk and Wanda moved closer to her. I figured that they were remembering the time when some men had tried to kidnap her—in the Case of the Vanishing Ventriloquist.

"That was a *question* I asked you, little girl," said the passenger, his smile less wide.

McGurk moved even closer to Mari and a little in front of her.

"Now just hold it," he said. "We've been warned about your kind."

The passenger raised his thick eyebrows as he turned to the driver.

"Hello, Roy! Another county heard from." He turned back to McGurk, the eyebrows down again. "And just what *is* our kind, sonny?"

McGurk's face flushed. If there's one thing he hates it's being addressed as "sonny."

"Strangers who come around striking up conversations with kids," he said.

"Huh!" grunted Stan. "Would it surprise you to know that we're government agents? Department of Justice. Immigration and Naturalization Service."

"Oh?"

McGurk looked a little taken aback.

"Yeah," said Stan. "And we're looking for an illegal

alien who's recently entered the country. From Tokyo, Japan. Name of Nakanishi."

"Which is why we're interested in *her*," said Roy, leaning forward and staring hard at Mari. "What *is* your name, little girl?"

"You have no authority to—" McGurk began.

"That is all right, Chief O'Rourke," said Mari. She smiled sweetly at the driver. "They call me Gimugimu, sir. Mari Gimugimu."

The men looked disappointed. McGurk spoke up again.

"How about *you* answering some questions now? Like how about showing us some ID?"

"We don't have to show our IDs to snot-nosed kids!" snarled Stan. "Beat it, sonny!"

Then Wanda piped up. Her eyes flashed as she tossed back her hair.

"If you *are* government employees," she said, "you've no right to talk to us like that! I'll see that our senator gets to hear of this!"

While she was letting rip, I'd gone around the back and was noting the car's number. Whether it was because Roy saw me doing this, or because of Wanda's words, I don't know. But without any further comment it was *they* who were beating it. Fast. Down the street and around the next corner.

"Did you get the number, Officer Rockaway?"

"Yes."

"Good. It may turn out to be very useful to the cops."

Wanda had turned to Mari.

"That was very good thinking," she said. "Giving them a false name."

"Oh, but it was not a falsehood!" said Mari. "My brothers *do* call me Mari Gimugimu. Sometimes."

"Oh?" I said.

"Yes," said Mari. "They tease me because I am always talking about my duty. As officer of the McGurk Organization. *Gimu* is Japanese for duty."

"Well, how about *that*?" said McGurk, grinning. Then he frowned slightly. "But what's all this Chief *O'Rourke* stuff? Something you caught off Patrolman Cassidy? Because it isn't *really* funny—"

"No, no, *no*, Chief McGurk!" said Mari. "I wasn't making fun! But you would not have wanted me to say your *real* name, would you? Something they could check on and look up in the phone book to find out where you live?"

McGurk was grinning again.

"Officer Grieg was right," he said. "*That* was very good thinking, too—Officer Gimugimu!" He turned. "Now let's get back to HQ quick, men. Before they come back!"

13 Yoshito's Ordeal

When we told Yoshito we'd just had an encounter with the two men, I thought he was going to dive under the table again. McGurk had to quickly order Wanda to lock the door and stand there on lookout. Yoshito's brush-tapping became faster and faster, as we told him what the men had said.

"Yes," he kept muttering. "They are the ones—yes, yes!" And: "Are you *sure* they didn't follow you?"

"Positive," said McGurk. "And now we really do have to know why they're so keen to get their hands on you. Otherwise we just can't handle your case. Okay?"

"Okay, okay!" said Yoshito. "I don't know much, but I will tell you what I *do* know."

So then he gave us the details that had us *all* feeling tense. I mean, now that we'd seen those guys, we could fully understand how scary it must have been for him.

When he'd left New York City in his rental car at seven o'clock the evening before, the only worry he had was about whether he'd get to the Yoshimura house in time for the meal at nine. And once he reached the last stretch of open country on the way to our town he was feeling fine.

"It was getting dark, but the route was clearly marked and it was only a few minutes past eight-thirty."

Which is when it happened.

He'd been aware that a car had been behind him for the last few miles. At first he wasn't bugged by it, but now that they'd reached a wooded area it had closed in and its headlights kept dazzling him. He slowed down from time to time to let it pass, but it slowed down, too.

And then suddenly someone in the car behind put a flashing light on the roof and it came up alongside. One of the occupants began to point to the side of the road.

"I thought it must have been the police. Maybe I have been speeding, I thought. Anyway, I was ready to apologize when I stopped and they stopped and both men got out. They *looked* like policemen."

"Yes," Brains agreed. "*I* thought they did, too. When—"

"Hold it," said McGurk. "Let the client tell it in his own words."

Brains nodded and Yoshito continued.

"They knew my name and this made me wonder if they were detectives who wished to ask questions about the *other* car. But then they told me what they told you. That they were immigration agents and did I have a work permit. I said yes, but that Hideo, our road manager, took care of all that. Then I began to wonder if they really were who they said they were."

Here Yoshito gulped and went into a terrific flurry of brush strokes.

"Why did you think that?" McGurk asked.

"Because—because one of them switched off the flashing light and the other took out a gun and said, 'You'd better come with us!' "

McGurk went perfectly still on the edge of his chair.

"*Arresting* you? At *gunpoint*?"

"Well, I guess I still thought they *had* to be government agents, so I moved toward their car to obey. But when the man with the gun said, 'No, not in there—in *there!*'—and he waved toward the trees, I knew then for sure that they weren't.

" 'We're going to take a little stroll,' he said. 'So walk.' Well, what could I do? I said, 'Here, take my watch, it is worth eighteen hundred dollars, and I have credit cards—' But he told me to shut up and keep walking. The other man had a flashlight, which he switched on after the first few yards. *He* seemed not so certain."

"Oh? How's that?" said McGurk.

"Because he said, 'You know what, Roy, I don't think he recognizes us after all.' And the man with the gun said, 'Maybe he's a good actor. Anyway, we can't take the risk.' And the other said, 'Well, at least use the silencer, just in case.' And then I knew."

"Knew what?" whispered Willie.

"I knew they were going to kill me."

Suddenly, Yoshito let the brushes fall and he sat back. In the dead silence, we stared at him.

McGurk was the first to speak.

"But why?" he said. "*Why* did—correction—do—*why* do they want to kill you?"

Yoshito made a long hissing noise through his teeth.

"I tell you I do not *know*! And I sure was not going to hang around and ask questions. So when I hear a clink and see the man begin to fit something to his gun, I acted fast. Thinking this is my only chance, I knocked the flashlight out of the other man's hand and ran— deeper and deeper into the wood, away from the path."

"Did—*did* they shoot?" asked Mari.

"Who knows? Maybe, with the silencer on. I heard only the crashing of the undergrowth as I ran and they ran. Also a voice saying, 'Hey, come back! We were only kidding!'—which I ignored."

"I should think so, too!" said Wanda.

"You keep watch on the outside, Officer Grieg!" McGurk reminded her. He turned to Yoshito. *"Then* what happened?"

"Then I kept very quiet and still, because the voice had seemed to come from farther away. And then I heard one of them say, 'Aw, come on, Stan. We know where he's headed anyway. And we know where he'll be at, all day Saturday, even if we don't catch up with him before then.' "

"So what did you do next?" asked Brains.

"I still kept quiet. It was only after I heard their car drive off that I began to make my way back to the road. Meaning to get back into my own car, of course."

"Ah!" McGurk began. "But—"

"I know, I know!" said Yoshito. "Dumb move! But then I think no. These men are very dangerous. One may be hiding in the back of my car."

"Exactly!" said McGurk. "That was *very* good thinking. So?"

"So I decided to abandon the car and only walked out onto the road much farther ahead. And when a pickup truck came along, I flagged it and told the driver that my car had broken down. I asked him for a ride to the nearest phone booth, which he did, bringing me to the outskirts of this town."

"And then you called the police, right?" said Willie.

"Well, no." Yoshito turned to Mari. "First, I phoned your father. And then, while we were speaking, I saw a silver-gray car going past on the other side of the road. It might *not* have been theirs, but I wasn't taking any chances. So I slipped into the nearest side street and kept on taking side streets until—well, you know the rest."

"But you *are* going to call the police?" said Mari.

"Well, no," he said, with an odd look—part hunted, part plain cussed. "Not yet."

"But they are trying to *kill* you!" said his cousin.

"I know that," said Yoshito, doggedly. "But—well—they may not be immigration agents—probably aren't—"

"Almost *certainly* aren't," I said. "Behaving like that! And whoever heard of a U.S. government agency using imported cars?"

"That's a point," McGurk murmured.

"But they *could* have found out something," said Yoshito.

"Like what?" McGurk asked sharply.

"Well," said Yoshito, "our road manager, Hideo, is very careless. He could have failed to obtain the correct work permits."

"So?" said McGurk, looking puzzled.

"So if my papers aren't in order when I go to report these men, the police will stop me giving my performance on Saturday." Yoshito turned to Mari. "And I have promised your mother I will do it!"

Mrs. Yoshimura is the local secretary for the Endangered Species Society. I mean, it was ironic really. Here was her famous nephew making *himself* an endangered species, just to keep his promise to her!

Mari obviously didn't think much of the deal.

"Oh, but the police will not be interested in your work permit," she said. "Not when you have something like this to report!"

But that cousin of hers was one stubborn guy.

"Oh, no?" he said. "In many of the countries we work in, that is one of the first things the police ask for."

"Yeah?" said McGurk. "Well, I don't think the cops work that close with other agencies in *this* country. Except maybe the FBI."

"And Hideo might *not* have been careless with your permits," said Mari.

"All the same, I cannot risk it," said Yoshito. "If I fail to keep my promise I shall never forgive myself. Never!" He shrugged. "*After* the gig, yes. *Then* I will report these men."

McGurk cleared his throat. He'd been looking very thoughtful.

"Yoshito," he murmured, "you said that at first you thought they were detectives, come to ask you about some other car. *What* other car?"

Yoshito shrugged again.

"Oh, it had nothing to do with this really."

"Look!" said McGurk. "You tell us you don't know why the men are out to get you, and I believe you. But at least you can tell us something you *do* know. Maybe *we* can figure it out. Now—what about this other car?"

That's when Yoshito told us about his previous rental, and how it had been stolen from the street outside his apartment the previous Sunday. He'd reported this to the rental company. But because he didn't really need a car for a few days, it wasn't until Wednesday afternoon that he'd gone around to pick up a replacement. Once again he was out of luck, however, when he found that the rental station had been burgled and burned down during the night.

"So I had to go to another firm," he said.

Well, it sounded as if Yoshito was right and it hadn't anything to do with the men in the Mercedes. But since it involved a crime in itself—two crimes in fact, maybe three—McGurk couldn't resist having me note the details. I later typed them up, because, as it happened, they did turn out to be important—*very* important—and here is a copy:

```
TIMETABLE RE STOLEN CAR:
Honda Accord (red) rented by
client Yoshito Nakanishi

SUN. June 21.  Car stolen from street (Riverside
Drive between 77th and 78th) between 6:00 P.M.
and 8:30 P.M.

8:45 P.M.  Theft reported to Econorentals
station, W. 75th.

WED. June 24.  Early hours, between 2:00 A.M. and
3:30 A.M., Econorental station burgled and
torched -- almost gutted.

1:30 P.M.  Yoshito discovers this when going
to rent replacement.
3:00 P.M.  Y. rents replacement from
another firm
```

But of course we didn't know the full importance *then*, late that Thursday morning.

"Well," said Wanda, when I'd finished jotting down the details. "I still think you ought to report the two men to the police, Yoshito."

"On Saturday," he repeated. "After the gig."

He looked so stubborn, none of us argued any further. Not even McGurk. In fact, I'm not sure *he* wasn't glad to go along with the client's wishes.

"Okay," he said to Yoshito. "Fair enough." And to us:

"So that's it, men. We have to make sure our client remains in hiding until Saturday." Then he *actually* rubbed his hands. "And, boy! Does the Organization have the facilities for *that!*"

At that moment, Mrs. McGurk shouted down to tell him his lunch was ready.

"What now?" said Yoshito, looking hunted again.

"You stay down here," McGurk said. "I'll sneak you something to eat later. You others better go get yours. I want you all back here by one-thirty. Then we'll decide exactly where to hide our client. Don't forget—it'll have to be for tonight and tomorrow night, as well as during the day. Hey, and be careful! Those guys could still be cruising around. Make sure you don't lead them *here!*"

On the way out, I took another look at the final results of the exercise. Just to have all the facts clear in my mind before coming to this momentous decision.

VITAL WITNESS PROTECTION EXERCISE			
Officer	Witness	Location	Length of time before discovery
McGurk	Dwight	Inside monster	43 hrs. 31 mins.
Rockaway	Fatso Sumo	Inside clothes closet	57 hrs. 15 mins.
Grieg & Yoshimura	Meryl	Tree house	25 hrs. 30 mins.
Sandowsky	Oswald	Garden shed	67 hrs. 30 mins.
Bellingham	John Doe	Loft space	10 hrs. 0 mins.

14 The Guy in the Monkey Suit

When I returned that afternoon, the others were already there, busy arguing. Wanda, who was back on lookout duty, hardly gave me a glance as she let me in.

"There's no contest!" she was saying.

"That's just *your* opinion!" said Willie.

The rest were all talking at once. All except Yoshito, of course. *He* was drumming away with his brushes, looking bewilderedly from one to another of us, and casting terribly anxious glances at the door.

After all, it was *his* fate the others were debating. The question of where he should hide during the next forty-four hours.

Then McGurk cut through the hubbub, slapping the table and saying, "The top priority has to be security!"

"Yes, but comfort shouldn't be ruled out," said Brains.

"With decent meals!" said Willie. "He can't go drumming nonstop all day Saturday on an empty stomach!"

McGurk slapped the table again, as the hubbub began to rise.

"Let's hear what Officer Rockaway has to say!" he declared.

Well, that was fine by me. I'd been giving a lot of thought to the problem over lunch. I had even made notes. These:

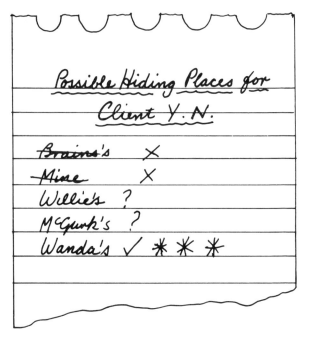

I put them on the table. The others clustered around.

"There you are!" said Wanda, pointing to the stars.

"Get back on task, Officer Grieg!" said McGurk, pointing to the door.

"Yes, you do that!" muttered Yoshito, mainly anxious about his *present* security.

"Talk us through your list, Officer Rockaway," said McGurk. "Give us your reasons. Starting at the top."

I looked at him suspiciously. I'd expected him to give me an immediate argument in favor of his own place. But he seemed to be regarding those stars very approvingly.

"First," I said, "all the hideouts in the exercise were well tested."

"Yes, and mine was the winner!" said Willie.

"Only under laboratory conditions," said Brains. "This time it has to be for real."

"Right," I said. "And one thing we all have going for us is that our families know about the exercise."

"You can say that again!" grumbled Brains.

"Which means that when we hide a real person," I said, "they'll think it's only another dummy."

"That's just what I've been saying," said McGurk.

"But *having* said that," I continued, "two are ruled out automatically. I mean, I don't see how we can smuggle Yoshito into Brains's house and up into the loft and expect him to stay there unnoticed."

"Not with the hole in the ceiling," said Brains, sadly.

"And we can't expect to hide anyone in my clothes closet for *that* length of time," I said.

I paused. I was coming to the difficult bit. Or so I thought.

"To hide him here, in McGurk's garage, inside the monster—well, I don't know," I said, bracing myself.

But he took it like a lamb.

"Forget it," he said. "Too risky. Garages are likely places for those guys to come investigating. Garages and—"

"Which leaves my shed," said Willie. "I mean—hey—who won the contest? And I can easily take him regular meals, and there's a recliner for him to sleep on, and—No?"

McGurk was shaking his head.

"Garages and *outbuildings*, I was going to say, Officer Sandowsky. Sheds like yours. And it was near your house that the men spoke to us this morning. They might have seen us coming out of your driveway."

"Which leaves the Treetop Hilton!" said Wanda, jubilantly. "Which has everything. Private bathroom, a sleeping bag, room-service meals at the pull of a rope, three-star recommendation by—"

"Cut the fooling, Officer Grieg!" said McGurk. "You know very well that what counts most is its top-security location."

"Yes," I said. "That was my thinking exactly. Even if the men did suspect he was up there, he'd be perfectly safe with the ladder pulled up. Long enough to raise the alarm, anyway."

Then Mari piped up.

"And we could make sure he had a supply of heavy weights, Chief McGurk! To hurl down at them! Rocks, too! And bottles filled with water to make them heavy!"

"Hey, yeah!" said Brains. "And why not filled with oil? *Boiling* oil? He could heat it up on a portable camping stove—"

"Don't get *too* carried away, Officer Bellingham! Rocks and plain heavy bottles should be enough."

Normally McGurk would have *loved* the idea of boiling oil. But—as he told us afterwards—this was a deadly serious situation requiring realistic practical measures.

I nodded.

"And as I say," I went on, "it would certainly raise the alarm."

"And give me time to call the police," said Wanda.

"Yes, but only if absolutely necessary!" said Yoshito, looking as stubborn as ever at the mention of calling the cops.

"So that's agreed, men," said McGurk. "We conceal our client in the hideout prepared by Officers Grieg and Yoshimura." He frowned. "There's just one problem."

"What's that?" asked Wanda, sharply.

"How to get him from here to there," he said. "Without risking being spotted."

Apart from a flurry of brush strokes, there was silence. Then:

"*I* know!" said Brains. "Why don't we take him inside

the monster? Like we were giving it a tryout for Saturday?"

"We-ell . . ." said McGurk, slowly. "That might attract too much attention."

"I'll *say* it would!" I agreed—thinking of that huge multicolored beast shuffling through the quiet afternoon streets.

"Now on Saturday," McGurk went on, "on the way to the parade, okay. People will expect to see something like that. On the other hand—"

He broke off. He was grinning and I knew that look. The jerk had had this great idea up his sleeve all along!

"On the other hand *what*, McGurk?" said Wanda.

"This," he said—and he went on to outline it and—well—it *was* a great idea.

Half an hour later, we were staring admiringly at the strange creature in our midst.

It was wearing Dwight's mask and cap, and at first sight it really did look gorilla-ish below the neck.

That was because it was covered with a rough-looking brown fur, all over its arms and body and most of its legs.

McGurk told us he'd already considered his mother's old fur coat for Dwight himself.

"I knew she wouldn't miss it," he explained. "It's only

imitation fur, but she used to get so many snide remarks from animal rights activists that she gave up on it. Dad sometimes uses it to cover the hood of the car in really cold weather."

"I wish it was really cold *now!*" came a faint voice from behind the mask. "I am sweating already!"

"That's okay, Yoshito," said McGurk. "As soon as you get into the tree house you can take it off. But no more talking, huh? I want people to think it's *me* in there."

I felt sorry for Yoshito. It wasn't as if he was wearing the long coat loose and flapping. We'd tried to make it look more like a regular gorilla suit by taping the skirts close around his legs, like pants. It must have been pushing 100 degrees Fahrenheit in there already!

McGurk fussed around as he saw us off, looking this way and that to make sure there was no silver-gray Mercedes in sight.

I suddenly felt kind of—well—touched.

"You sure you don't mind, McGurk?" I said, knowing how he liked to be in the thick of the action at all times. "I mean *I* could stay behind, then they'd think *I* was the one in the monkey suit."

He shook his head.

"No. It has to be me, Officer Rockaway. Someone folks would *expect* to see. Someone with—with a strong enough—uh—personality."

I could see what he meant. If the two men saw the bunch of kids with one dressed up like that, and they didn't see our leader with his flaming red hair and his pushy presence, they'd naturally expect he was the one inside that suit.

"Besides," he said, "I've got one or two phone calls to make, while Mom's out of the house."

15 The Missing Link

McGurk's instructions had been very clear.

"Proceed from here to Officer Grieg's by the shortest possible route. Not too fast, not too slow. Don't try to screen the client. Make like you're *proud* of the gorilla outfit—like it's gonna be another entry for the parade. Anybody asks, tell 'em it's the Missing Link. The creature that came between apes and man. And all the time keep your eyes peeled for those men. If they're anywhere around when you get near Officer Grieg's place, don't go in. Take another few turns around the block until they've gone. And Yoshito—you talk to no one. Got it?"

Well, for the first few hundred yards everything went according to plan. We saw no sign of the Mercedes. The few people we did pass just glanced at our monkey-suited companion and either grinned or scowled as if to say, "Oh, it's *them* again!"

Even Patrolman Cassidy was fooled. He was trimming his front hedge as we passed. He paused and nodded at Yoshito.

"Hi, McTurk!" he said. "You're looking good this afternoon!"

True to instructions, Yoshito made no reply.

Mr. Cassidy's grin only broadened, probably thinking McGurk hadn't liked his crack.

It was only when we got to the halfway mark that things began to get a little out of hand.

Yoshito stopped dead in his tracks.

"What?" said Wanda. "What's wrong?"

Yoshito grunted and pointed to the phone booth outside the pharmacy.

"For Pete's sake!" I whispered. "We can't be hanging around to make calls!"

But the eyes that peered out from the mask had that stubborn glint.

So we gathered around while the Missing Link made his call, hoping he'd keep his voice down.

"Aunt Akiko?" he murmured, when he got a reply.

"My mother!" gasped Mari.

"Yes. It is I—Yoshito," he was saying. "No—I cannot tell you right now. But I am fine. And I will definitely keep my date on Saturday. Just please go ahead with arrangements as planned, okay? I will explain everything then."

When he put the phone down, Wanda was mad.

"You go on like this and you *won't* be keeping your date on Saturday!"

"But this was necessary!" said Yoshito. "What would be the point of all this, please, if the gig was canceled due to my disappearance?"

"He's right," I said. "But let's—"

"Well, well, well!"

We spun around. Most of us knew that jeery sneery voice only too well. Sandra Ennis was just coming out of the pharmacy. She was walking kind of funny—two steps forward and one back, bobbing her golden curly head and wiggling her behind. I guessed she was practicing that dumb Dodo Dodder.

"You're always arguing with the jerk, Wanda," she said. "I wonder you don't break away and start your own Organization."

Then she stopped and looked our client up and down.

"Don't tell me, McGurk," she sneered. "You've given up on that stupid prehistoric monster and this is your new idea. Right?"

"Right," I said, glad she'd been fooled. So far, anyway. "He's the Missing Link. Half ape, half man."

"Huh!" she grunted. "*You* don't need fancy dress for that, McGurk. Why don't you come as you usually are?"

Thankfully, she's one of these creeps who make cracks like that and then run off before the victim can think of a reply. So she dodo-doddered off, tittering at her own joke.

"Come on!" Wanda growled to our hairy companion. "Before this ends in total disaster!"

But we got Yoshito to the Grieg yard without any further scare. There was still no sign of the Mercedes, and Wanda's mother was indoors, watching one of her favorite soaps. Even Ed was well out of the way, over at Jody Delano's place.

Therefore it was a cinch to get Yoshito installed in the tree house, with the rope ladder pulled up behind him.

One of the first things he did, I imagine, was take off that fur coat and let the sweat flow free. Then, when he let down the picnic box on the rope with a note on the scratch pad provided inside, asking room service for *Ice tea. Gallons of it!*—I judged it was time for us guys to leave the girls to it.

"Too many of us hanging around might attract attention," I said. "He's safe enough now."

"So long as they get the tea to him before he dies of dehydration," said Brains.

"He'll live," I said. "Anyway, let's go and report to McGurk."

He received our report without much enthusiasm. Even the fooling of Sandra Ennis didn't cheer him.

"If he hadn't stopped to make that call she'd never have seen him in the first place," he said.

"But it *was* a necessary call, as it turned out," I said.

"Yeah, I suppose so." He grunted.

"And what about *your* calls?" I said. "Did you get to make them?"

"Yeah, I made them."

"So—who to?"

"Well, first to directory assistance."

"Whose numbers did you want, McGurk?" asked Willie.

"First the Econorental place. Where Yoshito rented the stolen Honda. And that was a *complete* no-no. All I got was number unobtainable."

"Well, sure," said Brains. "The place was gutted in the fire."

"Yes," said McGurk testily. "But you'd think they'd have an *alternative* number. But I guess it was one of those cheap one-horse operations and that was the only station they had."

"What other place did you try?" I asked.

"The police, of course! The great N.Y.P.D.! The precinct in Manhattan where the Honda was stolen." McGurk sounded bitter.

"Well?"

"I was only asking what news they had about the stolen vehicle!"

"And?"

"All they could say was, 'Who wants to know?' And—

well—I didn't want to tell them about our client." McGurk sighed. "So I said I was asking for a friend who wished to remain anonymous. I even mentioned that it was a matter of *professional confidence*. But all the guy said was, 'Well, get him to call us himself!'—and hung up." He looked up with a kind of pleading expression. "Do—do I *really* sound like a kid, Officer Rockaway? Over the phone?"

"Well," I said, "I—uh—I suppose you do really. Why?"

"Because *he* called me 'sonny,' too!" he blurted.

"Anyway," said Willie, "why did you want to know about the stolen car, McGurk? It's the men in the Mercedes we're interested in, isn't it?"

"Yeah . . ." said McGurk, moodily. "But I still have a feeling there's some connection. If only I could put my finger on it."

16 Crisis in the Treetops

Wanda didn't show the next morning and Mari was late. She was breathless when she arrived.

"Wanda sends her apologies, Chief McGurk, but she is unable to come."

"Why?"

"It is Yoshito, Chief McGurk."

"What about him?" asked McGurk, suddenly alert. "Don't tell me he's fallen out of the tree!"

"No, no!" said Mari. "It—it is his drumming, Chief McGurk."

"What *about* his drumming?"

Mari sighed.

"Last night he ordered Chinese food. So Wanda got him some from the take-out. No problem. But—but she made mistake of sending it up complete with chopsticks."

"And?"

"And now he cannot resist using them for drumming. Ever since first light. On picnic box, on Pak-a-Potti, on hut walls. He cannot help it."

"So what's Officer Grieg doing about it?"

"She has to keep shouting up at him to be quieter. She dare not leave yard in case he breaks into really loud drumming."

"That's *all* we need!" groaned McGurk. "How come our clients are always such dummies?" He stood up. "I'd better have a word with him myself. I need to ask him a couple of questions, anyway."

"Can we all come?" asked Willie.

McGurk grunted. "Yeah, why not?" he said. "So long as we stay out of sight behind the bushes, we can continue our meeting there."

When we arrived, Wanda was in the front driveway talking to Mrs. Daly, their next-door neighbor. Our fellow officer looked relieved to see us. Everything seemed quiet enough up above, but she kept casting anxious glances in that direction.

"Phew!" she gasped, when Mrs. Daly had gone back in her house. "That was a close one!"

"Why?" said McGurk. "What happened?"

Wanda tossed back her hair.

"Yoshito pumping up the volume yet again is what

happened!" she said. "Beating the daylights out of the walls of the hut. I was yelling up at him to say for heavens' sakes, knock it off, will you, when Mrs. Daly came out. 'I'm surprised at you, Wanda Grieg!' she said. 'Hollering like that at the woodpecker!' "

She looked up, with a groan.

A thin *tink-tink-tink* was drifting down through the leaves. A red squirrel started joining in with its angry chattering.

"There he goes again!" said Wanda. "It sounds like it's only the plate, this time—but it'll soon get louder. Hey—you up there—keep the—!"

"Officer Grieg!" said McGurk. "You're making enough noise for *ten* drummers! Why don't you climb up and tell him—"

"I can't climb all the way up *every* time he starts getting too loud!" Wanda protested.

"No, not that," said McGurk. "I was going to say tell him I'm coming up myself to ask a few more questions. Then throw the rope ladder down for me."

"And while you're doing that, McGurk," said Brains, looking excited, "I'll run home and get something to solve Wanda's problem."

He arrived back, sweaty-faced and flushed, just as McGurk was climbing down. Brains was clutching a bunched-up length of thin cable and a cardboard box.

"What is it?" asked McGurk.

"Buzzer," said Brains. "Something I fixed up for my dad when he was in bed with laryngitis. So he didn't have to yell whenever he wanted something."

Ten minutes later, the gizmo was fixed, with the small loudspeaker up in Yoshito's hideout, the cable running down the tree trunk, hardly visible behind the leaves, and the bell-push wedged in the fork of a low branch.

"All you have to do is press it if Yoshito's drumming gets too loud," Brains said. "*He'll* hear the buzzer loud enough but no one else will."

"*Very* good thinking, Officer Bellingham!" said McGurk. "Now let's go around here, men. We have some serious questions to tackle."

So began the extraordinary meeting of the McGurk Organization in our temporary HQ behind the bushes, with us sitting in a close circle on the grass. From time to time, Wanda had to excuse herself while she buzzed Yoshito, but we were all very glad to see how well the device worked.

"Okay, McGurk," I said, when we were all sitting down. "What *were* your questions?"

"These," he said, handing me a crumpled piece of paper. "Concerning motives."

"*Yoshito's* motives?" said Willie.

"No," said McGurk. "The *men's* motives."

I was studying the list. The questions were jotted down *not* in his usual fancy curly writing, but in his scrawly hurried style. Hardly readable, full of crossings-out, weird spellings—a mess. But it was a good list and it certainly proved invaluable. So I typed it out later and here's a copy:

SPECIAL QUESTIONS PUT TO
CLIENT, June 26

Routine

    (a) Loan sharks out for repayment?
    (b) Protection racketeers?

Witness Theory

    1. Did you see them commit some crime?
    2. Did you see any crime being perpetrated lately by anyone at all?
    3. Did you witness the red Honda being stolen?
    4. Did you witness anything unusual that could have been a crime, if you'd only realized it at the time?
    5. Does some enemy want you to be killed? Some rival musician, maybe?

The answers to the routine questions were definitely negative—as McGurk had expected. So were the answers to #3 and #5. Yoshito hadn't seen the Honda being snitched. As for enemies wanting to kill him, that was ridiculous. Rival musicians don't want to kill each other *that* way, he told McGurk. Just to play so much better that the rival wants to crawl into a hole and die.

The answers to #1, #2, and #4 were also negative but less definite. If he *had* seen anything like that, he just couldn't recollect it.

"It looks like a clear case for hypnosis," said Brains.

McGurk looked at him hopefully.

"Have you been working on it lately, Officer Bellingham?"

Brains shook his head. He was looking reproachful now.

"No. Not after the time I tried to hypnotize *you*, McGurk."

Well, we knew what he meant. That had been one total flop. It nearly ended in Brains turning in his ID card. Perhaps one day I'll be able to reveal the grisly details. But not yet. Not here.

McGurk hastily changed the subject.

"It seems like it's the first case we ever had where the big mystery is not who did some crime but what crime did someone *do*?" He gave a baffled sigh. "And how come our client witnessed it without even knowing it?"

"Could it be that some other Japanese witnessed them committing a crime?" said Wanda. "And it's just mistaken

CRISIS IN THE TREETOPS / 121

identity?" She glanced apologetically at Mari. "You know how unobservant some people are. They think all Japanese look alike."

"Very true!" murmured Mari. "Same as all Americans do to some of *us*."

"Yes, but those guys knew his *name*," I said.

We all fell silent. Then McGurk folded his notes.

"Oh, well," he said, "we'll just have to keep plugging away. But, talking about being observant, there's something else. Tomorrow, after the show, when our client kindly releases us from our promise and we *can* go to the cops, we'll need to give a good description of those men. Don't forget—*we* saw them in broad daylight."

His face was bright and hopeful as he looked around at us. But within two minutes the freckles had bunched into one dark storm cloud.

I mean, we couldn't blame him really. Apart from the make of car and the fact that the men wore business suits, we couldn't agree on one single item. Some said Stan had blue eyes, others said gray. Some said it was Roy who had gray eyes and Stan's were brown anyway. We couldn't even agree on the colors of their suits and neckties.

I tell you, it was pandemonium for the next few minutes. Yoshito could have been banging and crashing away on his full drum kit and we wouldn't have heard.

Finally, McGurk raised his hand.

"Call yourselves detectives!" he said. "All you can agree on is they were wearing business suits and driving around in a Mercedes!"

"Well, *you* can talk, McGurk!" said Wanda. "You can't even be sure yourself!"

"*I* was too busy keeping the situation under control," said McGurk. "Challenging them for their IDs. You others had all the time in the world to look for scars, birthmarks—"

"I got their car number!" I protested.

"Yeah!" growled McGurk. "The car, the car! That's all you slobs can think of. But cars can be switched, sold, dumped, written off at any time. It's the *permanent* features we should—" He suddenly broke off. His eyes had narrowed. "Hey!" he drawled. "Wait a minute!" Then his face lit up. "That's it!" he yelled. *"That's it!"*

"What?" said Wanda.

"That's the missing link!"

"I do not follow, Chief McGurk," said Mari.

"Yoshito," he said. "Our client. What's the big difference between him and the dummies we practiced hiding?"

"He's alive," said Wanda. "And he drums."

The brisk *tink-tink* was getting louder. McGurk waved impatiently.

"No! I'm talking about the identities we gave the dummies. *He* isn't someone wrongfully accused of committing a crime, like Dwight. *He* isn't someone who witnessed a crime, like Meryl."

"But—"

"He's someone *wrongfully accused* of *witnessing* a crime! *He* didn't witness whatever crime it was the two guys committed. Someone else did."

"Who?" said Willie.

"Whoever stole his Honda!" said McGurk. "*That* was what the men would see when they realized they'd been spotted. Just a red Honda being driven away fast!"

"But—they have Yoshito's *name*," said Mari.

"Yes," said McGurk. "But let's stay with the guy in the stolen Honda. My bet is that they lit out after him even faster. And when he realized the Mercedes was soon gonna catch up, he dumped the Honda and made a run for it on foot, where they couldn't follow in their car. Across fields, down back alleys—who knows? It depends where the crime was committed."

"It *still* doesn't explain how come they knew Yoshito's name," said Brains.

"Oh, no?" said McGurk. "How about the abandoned Honda? Isn't that the first place they'd look, after they'd lost track of the driver? To see if there was a name tag on the steering wheel?"

"But it was a *rental*, McGurk!" said Wanda.

"Exactly, Officer Grieg! And *that* name—the Econorental name—was what they *did* find."

"Gosh!" I gasped. "The burglary, the fire—"

"Correct!" said McGurk. "The burglary to find Yoshito's name and address from the records. The fire to destroy any evidence they might have left while breaking in. Those guys must have been *really* desperate!"

We stared at him. It all seemed to figure.

Willie spoke first.

"So—uh—why didn't they kill Yoshito right away, McGurk? After they'd got his address?"

"In the city? In a busy apartment building? That would need very careful planning. These guys are pros. They'd have to make inquiries about Yoshito's movements. In fact, they probably started doing just that, that very morning. They probably found out from some doorman or janitor that Yoshito was due to be driving here later in the day, ready to give this performance on Saturday. He *is* quite famous, remember."

"Yeah," I said. "Didn't he say they mentioned knowing where he'd be on Saturday?"

"Right," said McGurk.

"Wow!" said Wanda. "What next, McGurk?"

"First," he said, "is your mom home?"

"No. She's having her hair done."

"Anyone else home?"

"No." Wanda glanced up at the tree, where the drumming was getting louder again. "Thank goodness!"

She stepped across and gave the buzzer a firm press.

"Great," said McGurk. "So it'll be okay if we use your phone." He turned to Mari. "Officer Yoshimura, are you in good voice today? I mean can you make it sound like you're a sober middle-aged person?"

"Well—yes, Chief McGurk. Sure."

"Terrific. So here's what I want you to say. . . ."

17 Mari Makes a Call

The telephone was in the Griegs' front hall. Mari held the receiver about an inch from her ear. That way we could just make out what the person at the other end was saying.

And let me say now that when she got through to the number McGurk himself had called yesterday, Mari's performance was tops. She sounded like one very businesslike forty-year-old.

"Good morning, young man. I am calling about the theft of a red Honda car, taken from Riverside Drive on—"

"Yes, ma'am," said the guy at the other end. "Do you wish to report it?"

"No, officer. That has already been done. It was stolen last Sunday afternoon. A red Honda Accord, owned by the Econorental company."

"Is *this* the Econorental—?"

"No. I am making a separate inquiry for my organization. Has the car been found yet?"

"Well, I can't tell you right off the bat, ma'am. If it's the one I'm thinking of, I believe it turned up someplace on Staten Island yesterday. Will you be the insurance company?'

Blandly, Mari ignored the question and asked one herself.

"Did you say Staten Island, officer?"

"Yes, ma'am."

At this stage, McGurk was making frantic, silently mouthed signs. Mari nodded.

"Do you know if a major crime was committed anywhere near where it was found?" she asked the cop. "Say within a half mile? Probably on Tuesday evening?"

The man's voice suddenly began to sound guarded.

"Well now, ma'am, this is taking us a long way from auto theft, isn't it? Did you say you were the insurers?"

Mari blinked.

"No, not exactly. But my organization is making inquiries. Merely routine, you understand."

The man hesitated. Then:

"Look, ma'am. If you'll just give me the name and phone number of your firm, I'll have the officer in charge of the case call you back. You are Ms.—?"

He paused, no doubt with pen at the ready. This time Mari lost some of her cool.

"I—oh—this is the"—she rolled her eyes pleadingly at McGurk, but he'd frozen—"the McGurk Organization," she said, taking the responsibility on her own shoulders.

Then she clamped her hand over the mouthpiece and whispered, "What number shall I give, Chief McGurk? Quickly!"

"Is that M-A-C Mac?" the cop was saying. "Or just M-C, ma'am?"

McGurk was still frozen, a look of sheer agony on his face. "Quickly!" Mari whispered again. He pointed desperately to the number on the dial.

"You can't give him *this* number!" hissed Wanda. "Mom will be back any minute!"

"But she can't give him *mine*!" croaked McGurk. "My mother will be sure to pick up the phone—even if we got back in time!"

"Maybe they won't call back for—" Brains began.

"Will you be quiet, Officer Bellingham? I'm—"

"Hello! Hello!" the voice was saying. "Are you still there, caller?"

Mari sighed.

"Yes—I am sorry, officer."

"Are those *kids* I can hear in the background, ma'am?" The voice had a suspicious ring now. "Because if they are, and this is some kinda school project, and you're their teacher, you should know better than—"

That was when Mari hung up. She had no choice. Wanda's mother was just opening the front door.

"Hello, what's all this?" she said, seeing us all clustered around the phone.

Mrs. Grieg wears those rimless glasses that make the wearer's eyes seem to bore holes in your head. McGurk had frozen up completely again. So had we all—except Wanda. *She'd* had plenty of practice, naturally.

"Oh, we were just checking something to do with tomorrow's drumming exhibition, Mom," she said. "Your hair looks great."

Those piercing eyes softened.

"Do you really think so?" said Mrs. Grieg. She even smiled as she turned to our voice expert. "How's your mother, Mari? Has the guest of honor turned up yet?"

If she'd only known it, the rattling, rapping woodpecker sound that came drifting in was answering her question!

"My mother is fine, Mrs. Grieg, thank you," said Mari. "And yes. Yoshito will definitely be coming to keep his promise."

"Sorry, Chief McGurk!" she said outside, while Wanda was giving the bell-push a savage jab. "I blew it, didn't I?"

"That's okay, Officer Yoshimura," he said, trying to hide his disappointment. "I guess we'll just have to go on handling this case alone, men."

But he's never one to sit around and mope. For the rest of the morning, he had us patrolling the neighborhood on our bicycles, looking for signs of the Mercedes— excepting Wanda, of course, who remained on duty under the Treetop Hilton. In the afternoon, we continued our patrol, this time without Mari as well. She had to help her mother prepare for tomorrow's big event at the Community Hall.

Again there was no sighting of the men.

"Maybe they've given up on Yoshito, after all," said McGurk. "Gone back to Detroit, or wherever they came from."

"The car had Illinois plates," I said. "Not Michigan."

"Anyway," said Brains, "I'm not so sure they *have* left the area. How about the car Yoshito abandoned Wednesday night?"

McGurk had been leaning heavily on the handlebars of his bicycle. Now he looked up sharply.

"What are you getting at?"

"Well, maybe that's where the men are concentrating their search," Brains said. "Hoping Yoshito will return to pick it up."

"Hey!" gasped Willie. "Yeah!"

McGurk was beaming again as he mounted his bike.

"Now that was *really* good thinking, Officer Bel-lingham!" he said. "We'd better check."

So we did—but cautiously, taking all the back roads and only going onto the main highway at the last possible point.

And, sure enough, there was Yoshito's car—another Honda Accord, but blue—over on the side of the road, where he said he'd left it. It looked like a lonely, sinister spot, near those trees, even in bright sunlight. After leaving our bikes in some long grass, we approached it very hesitantly.

"You're right, Officer Bellingham," said McGurk, when we got up close. "I bet they *are* using it as bait."

"Why so sure?" I said.

"It's locked. *Now* it is. But I bet it wouldn't have been when they took him into the trees."

"Well, who *did* lock it then?" said Willie.

"*They* must have," said McGurk. "So it wouldn't at-tract attention. So anyone seeing it would just think it had broken down and was left here until it could be fixed."

"Why would the men be so concerned?" I said, making a note of the license number, out of habit.

"So there wouldn't be a general alert, of course," said McGurk. "About a missing driver. They want him for themselves. Yes. You're right, Officer Bellingham. This is where they'll have been waiting for him to show."

Willie gulped.

"Well—they don't seem to be anywhere around *now*."

"No," said McGurk. "But they might not be very far away. Let's continue our surveillance from the trees, men."

We waited about an hour, but there was still no sign of them, so we picked up our bicycles and went back the way we had come. Personally, I felt very subdued by this further evidence of the men's patience and cunning. I mean, all right, they hadn't showed while we were in hiding. But who was to say they, too, hadn't been concealed? Someplace farther along the road, perhaps, where they could keep an eye on the car through binoculars?

Or—I nearly fell off my bike when this occurred to me—*or keeping an eye on the car through telescopic sights?*

I didn't say anything about this to the others. They were looking pretty subdued themselves. And McGurk was no longer talking about the possibility of the men abandoning their hunt for Yoshito.

A few hours later, we heard the news that clinched it. Mari broke it in a phone call to McGurk just after nine, and he phoned it through to me.

"She says they're definitely still around. She's seen them with her own eyes."

"Where?"

"She was just leaving the Community Hall with her mother. Mrs. Yoshimura had been making some last-minute arrangements. And all of a sudden, there it was— the silver-gray Mercedes, slowly gliding around the next corner. She recognized the driver, under the street-lights. She thinks they were casing the Community Hall and so do I. Ready to make their move tomorrow. . . ."

18 The Last-Minute Arrival

Our leader's plan for getting Yoshito to the parade the next morning was simple.

McGurk, Brains, Mari, and Willie would travel inside the monster (himself up front, of course), while I would walk on the outside, by its great grotesque head. This was partly to make sure the beast didn't blunder into anything, and partly so there'd be at least one pair of eyes free to watch out for the men in the Mercedes.

The next stage was to stop by at the Grieg yard and pick up Wanda and our client.

Well, all this went without a hitch. My heart was pumping a little faster as I led the swaying monster into the driveway, but I needn't have worried. Wanda and Yoshito were already waiting in the bushes next to the sycamore tree. Nobody had spotted Yoshito climbing down the rope ladder, and even if they had, they wouldn't have been able to recognize him because of the gorilla mask.

"He refuses to wear the fur coat, though," said Wanda, as the monster shambled up to them.

"No way!" said the gorilla. "Not with a whole day's drumming ahead!"

"And I don't blame him," said Wanda. "The sun's getting hot already."

"Cut the yacking and get inside!" grumbled the McGurkosaurus.

As I mentioned at the beginning, this was one very roomy monster. When McGurk hoisted up the front part and Wanda and Yoshito had stepped inside, they were soon swallowed up. The only difference was that the creature now had twelve active feet instead of eight, and they didn't all go in the same direction sometimes. But I managed to steer them safely to the marshaling point, where the fire department's marching band was already tuning up.

Then it became a parade proper. I won't go into too much detail here, except to say that it was pretty impressive as parades go, with some entries almost as spectacular and/or crazy as our own.

Like Sandra Ennis, all fluffed up with gray feathers and a big curved false beak, doing her doddering in time with the band. And Burt Rafferty's and Tommy Camuty's shaggy-rug mammoth, which was only spoiled when its ox-horn tusks started slipping. There were floats, too. The Boy Scouts had come as a party of big-game hunters, with solar helmets and rifles and riding breeches, representing one reason why so many animals were becoming extinct. The Girl Scouts had constructed a prehistoric diorama for their float, with papier-maché monsters. A bit dull and static, maybe, but with everything exactly to scale, *including* a stegosaurus. Brains raved about it later, when he got to see it properly.

Not that *I* was paying much attention. I was much more concerned to keep an eye on the sidewalks, where the crowd was getting thicker the closer we came to the Community Hall. The route had been closed off to ordinary traffic, but as far as I could see, the two men weren't hanging around on the sidewalk, and for that I was mightily thankful. Also for the fact that there were a couple of police cars, one at the head of the parade and one at the rear.

This was just routine, of course. At that stage, the last thing the cops themselves were looking for was a pair of armed and murderous hoods. But at least it would make it less likely for the men to take any action yet—even if they recognized Yoshito's feet among the other ten.

I hoped so, anyway.

It was about 9:45 when we reached the judging point, outside the Community Hall. And since much of what happened from then on was to take place inside that building or its grounds, I have borrowed the plan I made of it for the Vanishing Ventriloquist case notes.

This one:

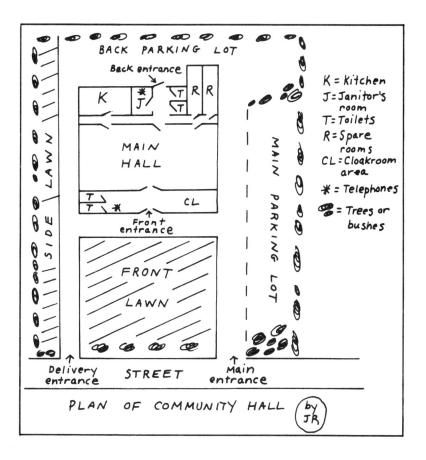

BACK PARKING LOT

Back entrance

K

J

T
T

R R

MAIN
HALL

T
T *

CL

Front
entrance

FRONT

LAWN

SIDE LAWN

MAIN PARKING LOT

Delivery
entrance

STREET

Main
entrance

K = Kitchen
J = Janitor's
room
T = Toilets
R = Spare
rooms
CL = Cloakroom
area
* = Telephones
= Trees or
bushes

PLAN OF COMMUNITY HALL (by JR)

Well, the judges were standing on the edge of the lawn, just in front of the bushes, facing the street. The mayor was there, along with Mari's mother and several other members of the Endangered Species committee. The mayor was all smiles as the parade passed slowly in front of him, then came to a halt. Mrs. Yoshimura didn't look too happy, though.

While the mayor told us what a great turnout it had been, and how very hard he'd have to think before he could finally announce the winner at six o'clock, Mrs. Yoshimura kept casting worried glances up and down the street. Finally, when the mayor was through, she whispered something in his ear.

His face clouded. Then he cleared his throat and said to the crowd, "I—uh—understand the guest of honor has been delayed. But I'm sure—"

He broke off, gaping, as the McGurkosaurus shuffled up, thrust its huge ugly head at Mrs. Yoshimura, and said, "It is okay, Aunt Akiko. I am in here!"

And then, gruffly, in another voice, "Yeah, but he doesn't step out until he's safely at the door. Come on, men!"

Whereupon, to everyone's astonishment, the monster marched straight up through the delivery entrance, cut across the lawn, and came to a halt against the front doors.

"Hey!" yelled the mayor, as McGurk and the others clambered out from under. "What *is* this?"

But when McGurk bundled Yoshito through the doorway and our client took off his gorilla mask, everything became clear.

"You had us very, very worried!" said Mrs. Yoshimura, shaking her head but smiling. "We thought you would never arrive!"

"I promised, didn't I?" said Yoshito, all smiles himself. "But these are the guys you have to thank, really. As you will find out later, when I explain."

"Nothing to it, ma'am!" said McGurk, with a *very* immodest smirk. "And now, if you'll excuse us, we'd better park our model around the back somewhere."

But Mrs. Yoshimura wouldn't hear of it.

"Why don't you leave it on the front lawn?" she said. "It may not be very—ah—authentic, but it is so colorful and eye-catching! It will make a marvelous sign for any stranger who might not be sure where the Endangered Species drumming exhibition is."

So that's where we parked it.

And, boy, what a lucky break *that* was to turn out to be!

It didn't take long for Yoshito to swing into his stride.

The town's music store had loaned the sponsors a complete full-size drum kit, and the moment our client spotted it, his eyes lit up. Even while the committee secretary was introducing him, Yoshito was crouched down, tisk-tisking away on the cymbals. The tisking grew into a brisk chink-chinking as the secretary was pointing out the table in the corner where pledges could be made—anything from five dollars upwards, to be paid if Yoshito completed his twelve-hour nonstop session successfully. And when the man read out the rules—like Yoshito having to take a pair of cymbals or a triangle with him if he had to go to the bathroom—his beats got steadier and louder.

Well, we knew what he could do with just a couple of chopsticks, a few plates, a picnic box, and a portable john, but this was something else. He seemed to pick up inspiration with every stroke. The crowd was soon cheering and stamping. It became obvious that a lot of amateur drummers had come along, eager to pick up tips, and Yoshito wasn't disappointing them. Some began to call out requests, asking for things like "single-stroke rolls," and "rim shots," "ratamacues," and "flam paradiddles."

He obliged them all. We began to feel quite proud of him. And everyone was enjoying it, not just the experts. In the first half hour the pledge number had passed the $500 mark and was rising.

Someone from the local radio station interviewed him as he played on. He courteously kept it soft, on the cymbals mostly, as he listened to and answered the questions, but he never missed a beat. It was the same when a reporter from the daily paper came.

"Shouldn't *we* pledge something?" asked Wanda, starry-eyed. "Out of the Organization slush fund?"

It was just turning eleven and the display board was registering $950.

McGurk refused.

"If it wasn't for us, there'd be no pledges at all!" he said.

Mari had been very quiet up until this point. She'd obviously been feeling increasingly anxious.

"Maybe we should be reporting those men to the police now, Chief McGurk," she said. "In case they come to kill him *during* the exhibition."

McGurk looked around at the crowd.

"My guess is that they won't try anything yet," he said. "Not with all these witnesses."

"Let's ask Yoshito again," said Wanda, looking doubtful. "After all, it's *his* life."

But when we went up close and put our question to him over a soft spell on the cymbals, Yoshito wouldn't hear of it.

"No," he murmured. "Please, no. If you tell the police now they will want to question me. Then I will be made to break off and all pledges will be canceled." He pointed with one of his sticks at the indicator board, which had just registered $1,000. "Tonight—ten o'clock—*then* I will report to police."

And as if to underline this, he crashed and clashed into a prolonged explosive bout of drumming that raised cheers from the crowd and sent the pledge figures jumping to $1,250 in less than five minutes.

"He's right, men," said McGurk. "Besides, if there's one thing those two guys are *not*, it's reckless. They aren't terrorists. *They* wouldn't come in shooting and take their chances about making a getaway. They're cool professional killers. . . . No. The danger time will be after ten, when most of the crowd's gone home and it's—"

"Hello!" said Wanda. "I wonder what Mr. Cassidy wants?"

We turned.

The policeman looked grave as he stood in the doorway, surveying the crowd. And we were soon in no doubt about what he wanted, as he threaded his way toward us.

"McGurk," he said (and *that* showed how serious he was, using our leader's correct name), "you others, too— you better come with me. Now. Lieutenant Kaspar wants to speak with you, and it's urgent."

19 The Collar

Our monster looked very colorful in the sunlight as we followed Patrolman Cassidy. There was no sign of his patrol car, though. Only a plain black van, parked in the street. It had darkened glass windows at the sides and back.

"Isn't this a—?" I began.

"Patrol wagon, yes," said Mr. Cassidy. "Also known as a paddy wagon or Black Maria."

"But—that's for transporting *prisoners*!" said McGurk.

"Correct!" said Patrolman Cassidy, opening the back doors. "Get in!"

That was a big enough shock in itself. But when we saw Lieutenant Kaspar glowering at us, and a man with him looking almost as stern and disapproving, my heart gave another lurch. They certainly hadn't sent for us to wish us a nice day.

There were two long bench seats, one along either side. The men were sitting on a couple of jump seats at the far end, facing the door.

"Hurry up and sit down!" snapped Lieutenant Kaspar. "And close the door, Cassidy. This isn't a sideshow."

Despite the dark window glass, it was quite light in there. Lieutenant Kaspar's face was flushed a bright pink—sure sign that he was annoyed—and his blue eyes shone fiercely. The other man was a complete stranger. He was wearing a crumpled lightweight brown jacket with a yellow silk handkerchief spilling out of the breast pocket. He was very dark-skinned, with brown eyes.

"This is Lieutenant Gonsalves," said Lieutenant Kaspar. "N.Y.P.D."

The stranger was frowning as he looked at us.

"Is *this* the—the McGurk Organization?" he said.

"That's what they call themselves, yes," said Lieutenant Kaspar. "And that one with the red hair is McGurk."

"The head of the Organization, sir," said McGurk. "And these are my officers. Officer Joey R—"

"Be quiet!" said Lieutenant Kaspar.

Lieutenant Gonsalves was giving us another looking-over.

"So *you're* the kids who were inquiring about a red Honda Accord that had been taken without the owner's consent?"

"Uh—yes, sir," murmured McGurk.

"And who, may I ask, was the adult you got to speak for you?" said the New York cop. "The woman?"

"I, sir," said Mari, in a dry hushed voice.

"*You?*"

"Our voice expert, sir," McGurk began. "She—"

"She *does* have some kind of gift for imitations," said Lieutenant Kaspar, giving Mari and McGurk a scowl each. "They're telling the truth. They always do—finally."

Lieutenant Gonsalves turned back to us.

"Okay. Then you are not denying you made a phone call to the precinct at ten-thirty-five A.M. yesterday?"

"With a query that wasn't picked up by the officer in charge of the case until eleven P.M.," cut in Lieutenant Kaspar. "Who then spent most of the night trying to track down some *regular* firm calling themselves the McGurk Organization!"

He spoke bitterly. As we found out later, it wasn't until around 8:30 that morning that the inquiry about the elusive firm reached him, just as he was beginning a leisurely Saturday breakfast.

After Lieutenant Kaspar had gotten that off his chest, the N.Y.P.D. man continued his interrogation, asking how *we* knew about the red Honda and why we'd been so interested to know if it had been found.

McGurk was now looking much more like his usual confident self. He told the cop about Yoshito's appeal for help, and the men who were looking for him, and our promise to hide him.

Neither of the lieutenants interrupted this time. They even seemed to be holding their breath when McGurk was talking about the two men.

Not until McGurk had brought them up to date, telling them how we'd safely delivered Yoshito to the hall, did Lieutenant Kaspar speak.

"Why didn't he report it to *us*?"

McGurk explained that, too—careful to point out that we had urged Yoshito to do just that.

Lieutenant Kaspar only grunted with disgust, making it pretty clear that his opinion of the general public wasn't all that different from McGurk's opinion about clients.

But Lieutenant Gonsalves obviously had more pressing things on his mind.

"So what was this query about a possible major crime near where the Honda was found?" he asked.

This time McGurk sounded not merely confident but positively and obnoxiously triumphant as he told them of his hunch.

Lieutenant Gonsalves looked very impressed.

"That's just about right," he said to Lieutenant Kaspar. "It looks like these two guys are the Staten Island killers, after all."

"The—the Staten Island killers, sir?" whispered McGurk.

The cop hesitated, then shrugged.

"Yes," he said. "You deserve to know, I guess. But on Tuesday night, in a parking lot less than half a mile from the abandoned Honda, a reputed mobster was found slumped over the wheel of his car with a bullet hole in the back of his head."

He paused. In the silence, I could hear drumming and cheering noises floating from across the lawn and over our monster.

"The car thief," Lieutenant Gonsalves continued, "a punk with a long joyriding record, witnessed the whole thing. He'd been parked in the same lot, catching a nap, with the seat full down, out of sight. When he realized what was happening, he panicked and drove off like a bat out of hell. Like you figured."

McGurk's broad smirk slowly subsided as the cop continued.

The abandoned Honda hadn't been spotted until Thursday, he told us. And even then the police hadn't connected it with the shooting. It was only when the joyrider's fingerprints were found all over it and he was pulled in on Friday morning that the truth began to emerge.

"At first he tried bargaining. Saying that if we dropped the auto charge he might be able to help us with something really big. And—well—it wasn't until nine last night that he told us about the killing. Then it was another couple of hours before someone told me about the crazy call that had come in midmorning from someone calling themselves the McGurk Organization."

"How about *that*?" murmured McGurk, glancing at us triumphantly.

"Anyway," said Lieutenant Kaspar, "it looks like these two guys *are* the perpetrators, right enough."

"No doubt in *my* mind," said Lieutenant Gonsalves.

"Shall I go get the drummer, sir?" said Patrolman Cassidy.

Lieutenant Kaspar shook his head.

"Why bother?" he said. "He's safe enough for the time being. I have a strong feeling they won't be making their move until the end of the exhibition."

"Me, too, sir!" said McGurk.

"We can't be *sure* of that," said the New York cop.

"I know," said Lieutenant Kaspar. "But we'll probably have collared them long before then. There can't be all that many silver-gray Mercedeses in the vicinity."

"Especially with this number," I said, flipping through my notebook. I passed it to Lieutenant Gonsalves, who'd reached out. "Illinois registration, see?"

"Illinois?" he said, frowning. "This is a *New York* number."

I grabbed it back.

"Sorry!" I said. I'd given him the number of the blue Honda we'd found yesterday. "Different car." I flipped

THE COLLAR / 149

the pages. *"This* is the Mercedes."

"Do you *mind*?" said Lieutenant Kaspar, impatiently. He took the notebook, tore out the page, and handed it to the patrolman. "Have this relayed to all cars. Top priority. Good work!" he said, giving me back my notebook.

At first I thought McGurk was miffed because I'd just been praised for something *he'd* been so scornful about yesterday. But it was something else.

"Lieutenant Kaspar . . . ?"

"Yes?"

"You just said they'd be planning to come and get Yoshito after the exhibition," said McGurk.

"I also said we'd probably have picked them up long before then."

"Yes," said McGurk. "But if you don't, and if they slip through your net and maybe come on foot, you'll need *us.* I mean we're the only ones who've had a good look at them and—and—"

Lieutenant Kaspar's face had been turning a deeper shade of pink. He started wagging his finger.

"If you're suggesting you join a police stakeout, outside the Community Hall, after dark, for two armed and dangerous criminals—*you*, a bunch of minors!—well—" He took a deep breath. "How d'you think your *parents* would feel about that? Huh?"

"But I know the perfect place to keep watch from—"

"I don't care if you know *twenty* perfect places!" Lieutenant Kaspar thundered. "You stay well away from here at that time, you understand? Now get off back to the exhibition and enjoy your friend's drumming. Lieutenant Gonsalves and I have a lot of planning to do."

He slid open the window behind him, where Mr. Cassidy had been transmitting his message. As we left, we heard the lieutenant say, "Drive around to the back parking lot, out of the way."

McGurk began sounding off as we made our way back up the driveway, behind the wagon.

"How d'you like that guy? If it wasn't for us they wouldn't even know what kind of a car to look for! And all we get is the brush-off! 'Bunch of *minors*!' It's a wonder *he* didn't call me sonny!"

"What *was* the perfect place, McGurk?" asked Willie.

"Huh?"

"The perfect place to look out for them from?"

"Oh"—McGurk brightened up—"That!" he said, pointing to the McGurkosaurus.

"Our monster?" said Wanda.

"Sure. With a few more eyeholes punched in its sides, we'd have a complete three-hundred-sixty-degree view. Every approach to the hall—Come on, men. I'll show you now. Have you got your knife, Officer Bellingham?"

Well, it *was* our model, and we *did* have permission

to park it there. So we didn't bother about anyone seeing us getting back inside it.

And when Brains had punched the extra eyeholes with his new Swiss Army knife, some of us began to feel as regretful as our leader.

"You're right, McGurk." Wanda sighed, peeking through one of the holes. "It *would* be a perfect place."

"You bet it would!" he said. "They'd never even dream they were being kept under observation from here!"

"*I* have the whole of the service driveway covered, Chief McGurk," said Mari.

"And I could keep an eye on the front entrance itself," said Brains.

"This would give *me* a pretty good view of the street," murmured Willie.

"And I'd be able to see anyone coming up the—"

I was going to say "main driveway," but I stopped, hardly able to believe my right eye. "It—it *can't* be . . ."

"Can't be what, Officer Rockaway?"

"The blue Honda! The one Yoshito had to abandon! With the New York number, see! And now it's *here*! Just moving into the parking lot. With *them* in it!"

It's a miracle the monster didn't tilt over onto its massive snout, there was such a rush to my end. Then:

"Gosh!" murmured McGurk. "You're right!"

One by one, the others took a peek and agreed.

It was the two killers, right enough, sitting there as cool as you please. They were making no move to get out, I was relieved to note.

"They must have stashed the Mercedes somewhere out of sight," I said. "The highway cops'll be wasting their time. None of them will think of watching for *this* car!"

"I told you, men," McGurk said, grimly, "this is one cool pair of professionals!"

"But what are they doing *here*?" asked Wanda. "Right *now*?"

McGurk grunted. "Just giving the place a double check, I guess. Seeing what kind of police presence there might be."

"You—you don't think they might be going to get Yoshito now, do you?" Willie asked.

"With guys like that, who knows?" said McGurk. "Listen. Officer Bellingham—you're about the smallest and—uh—least memorable. Do you think you could crawl out from under the monster's tail, on their blind side?"

"*Me?*" gasped Brains.

"Yes, you. And then sort of casually stroll around to the back and tell Lieutenant Kaspar just who *this* bunch of minors is keeping under surveillance at this very moment in time!"

"But what if those guys recognize me?"

"Here," said McGurk, taking something from under his shirt. "Put this on if it makes you feel better."

It was the folded-up gorilla mask.

Well, I guess it *must* have made Brains feel better. Without any further argument, he put on the mask and set out on his mission.

I turned back to my spyhole.

The men were laughing. Maybe about how they'd hoodwinked the cops. They weren't looking in our direction.

So we waited, hoping the men wouldn't decide to move off before Brains could deliver the message.

"He must be taking his time," murmured Wanda, after two or three minutes.

"If anyone is taking their time it won't be *my* officer," said McGurk. "But since he's only a *kid*, who knows how fast Lieutenant Kaspar will be responding to him?"

He spoke bitterly, but he needn't have worried. Even before the last word was out of his mouth, I saw a patrol car slide silently into view at the end of the driveway, blocking it off.

Then Wanda gasped. "Here comes Lieutenant Gonsalves from around the back!"

I switched eyeholes just in time to see the New York cop walk slowly in front of the Honda, put a cigarette in

his mouth, stop, fumble in his pockets as if for a match—
then suddenly straighten up with a gun in one hand and
his badge in the other.

At the same instant, two more cops dashed to the
scene, also with guns at the ready: Patrolman Cassidy
from the top of the driveway, the other cop from the car
at the end.

The two hoods didn't have a chance.

By the time we emerged from the bowels of the monster, those guys were pressed face down against the Honda's roof, having their hands cuffed and their rights read.
Lieutenant Kaspar, already on the scene, was gazing
down at two ugly-looking handguns that had been laid
on the hood, partly covered by Lieutenant Gonsalves's
yellow silk handkerchief.

"Good work—uh—McGurk," murmured Lieutenant
Kaspar, rather grudgingly, perhaps.

"*Very* good work!" said Lieutenant Gonsalves. "All of
you! If you're ever looking for jobs when you leave
school, be sure to let us know at the N.Y.P.D."

"Will do!" said McGurk, positively glowing. Then he
frowned. "But I have to warn you, sir. When I'm captain
of my own precinct, I'll be making a strict new rule."

"Oh?" said Lieutenant Gonsalves. "What's that?"

"I'm gonna demand the badge and gun of every duty
officer who doesn't take calls from kids seriously!"

20 Rewards—and Punishments

After that, it was a day of good news and bad news.

The good news first.

When Yoshito heard about the arrest of the hoods, his drumming became even more spectacular. "A paean of percussive joy," as the local newspaper's music critic called it. The result was a pledge total of over $15,000.

The bad news was that at six o'clock, when the judges announced their verdict, we did *not* win first prize. The Girl Scouts won that with their diorama. We got an honorable mention, sure—for one of the best *fun* entries! And even that distinction had to be shared with the Boy Scout big-game hunters and—are you ready for this?— Sandra Ennis's dodo.

Normally, McGurk would have protested, crying, "Foul!" and "Fix!" and stuff like that. But today, with the Organization's triumph still uppermost in his mind, he couldn't have cared less. After all, it was *our* model the TV crew took most shots of that evening. It was only because of its police news value, of course, but that didn't worry our leader, as he posed with it on the lawn, pointing to the spyholes and putting it through its paces, with the rest of us out of sight inside it—doing all the legwork, as usual.

And later, in the following days and weeks?

Well, the two men are still awaiting trial. But there seems to be no doubt about *their* fate. Being hired killers, they'll probably have many more charges of cold-blooded murder to answer to. And Patrolman Cassidy has told us confidentially that they're certain to be facing more than a dozen life sentences *each*!

As for their *intended* victim, Yoshito couldn't thank us enough. The Asamayama band is to give a big concert in Central Park, in New York, later this summer, and guess who'll be the guests of honor *this* time?

You've got it. Mr. and Mrs. Yoshimura are hiring a bus to take us all down there, plus any young members of our families who care to go along. Wanda isn't any too pleased about that, because Ed has muscled in, together with Jody Delano. But—hey!—*she* should worry. *I'm* going to be lumbered with Cousin Benny!

Anything else?

Oh, yes—McGurk has taken to carrying around a huge yellow silk handkerchief. He says it's an essential part of a police officer's equipment. For handling any possible murder weapon and preserving the fingerprints, would you believe!

I mean, the fact that we've now successfully dealt with the biggest crime of all has really gone to his head. You only have to look at the latest addition to the list of our achievements at the foot of the McGurk Organization notice.

"It calls for a real double-decker!" he insisted, when he asked me to type it.

And here it is:

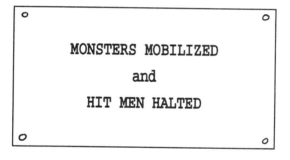

```
o                                          o


         MONSTERS MOBILIZED

                and

          HIT MEN HALTED


o                                          o
```